The BOOB Girls X

10/18

The Burned Out Old Broads at Table 12

Gospel Bird

A Novel by Joy Johnson

To order make checks payable to Joy Johnson Brown,
7230 Maple St, Omaha, NE 68134

Phone: 1-866-218-0101

Dedication:

This book is dedicated to the Reverend Doctor James Campbell. Known to me as Slik. Friend for more than half my life, fellow wordsmith, creator of crazy names, plotter of plots and my go-to muse. Jim's Hemorrhoid sermon is in book II and another sermon is in this one. Jim has written: ***To Follow the Cabbage – the real story of Alaska, The Secret Places***-childhood grief, ***The Holiness of Water***- a beautiful book about water and Christianity, ***What do You Say?*** – communicating with nursing home residents, ***The Chair*** – go cross-country with a chair strapped on top of a car, and Jim painted the fabulous picture of "The BOOB Girl Birds."

Keep your powder dry, old friend.

BOOBs X is also in memory of BOOB Girl pioneer in so many ways, Mildred Woolley.

BOOB Birds Print Full Color

Unframed, 18x24

$25

Order from www.theboobgirls.com or

www.centering.org

Phone: 1-866-218-0101

Part One
Prologue

From The BOOB Girls: The Musical: the girls meet Wiley Vondra, the naked man in the laundry room and he invites them to a game of poker. Hadley asks if it's strip poker and she's glad she's still wearing her earrings.

Wiley's Song: ***None of that Kinky Stuff***

I like a nice clean game, slow paced,
no wild cards and no flirts.
You gotta keep your poker face
or you might just lose your shirt.

I've traveled through the wide, wild west.
I've seen a thing or two.

The girls who had me most impressed were
sturdy, smart and true.
But when a wench would come my way with
fancy city ways to play
I'd always turn to her and say,

None of that kinky stuff, none of that kinky stuff.
Just keep your weirdness to yourself.

None of that kinky stuff.

Like riding crops and leather straps. None of
that kinky stuff.
No body paints or rubber chaps.
None of that kinky stuff.

No bathtubs filled with Jello mix.
None of that kinky stuff.
No caramel sauce with ready whip.
None of that kinky stuff.

And when you've shared and bared it all you'll
see the time has come
The sunset makes the shadows tall,
and the game of cards is done.

But if our paths should cross someday,
Now don't be shy and don't delay,
Just go on, turn to me and say,

None of that kinky stuff, none of that kinky stuff.
Just keep your weirdness to yourself.
None of that kinky stuff.

Two Tragic Stories

"We're going to Alaska!" Marge Aaron said, slamming down a three-page letter onto table 12.

"No we're not," three voices echoed as one.

Silence.

Marge stood up, her bad knee popping in protest, her red cane swinging and nearly falling off the back of her chair.

Geoffrey, their oversized mastiff, raised his head. "Go," was one of his favorite words. This one might involve ice cream. He was the only one listening intently. He had perked up ears, he wasn't moving. Geoffrey was in his favorite spot; curled up under table 12 in such a way that his big, awkward body was touching the feet of every one of his women seated above him.

Doggie Heaven.

Alphonso Greatwood and Wiley Vondra, who were playing checkers at the table next to the girls, weren't listening. In fact, no one seemed to even notice that Marge was standing. Hadley Joy Morris-Whitfield was reading a James Hankins novel on her tablet, Robinson Leary was, as usual, bent into her laptop researching her current intellectual love interest; Apache Culture, and Mary Rose McGill was making a valiant attempt to master her new crossword puzzle app on her smart phone. Mary Rose also had an app simply called, "Poop", which kept track of certain elimination habits, but she hadn't used that one for some time.

"Hey, Everybody!" Marge said loudly, clapping her hands. "We have to go to Alaska!"

"We already said we didn't." Robbie said, not missing a key stroke on her computer.

Wiley Vondra didn't miss a checker move, either, though both he and Alphonso had jumped a little when Marge clapped her hands.

"What did Dela-ware to the Iditarod?" he asked.

Alphonso made his next move without looking up either, "I dunno," he said, "Al-aska," and still without looking up, they gave each other a high five.

Wiley finally looked over the board at Alphonso. "Alaskans have more mileage on their snow blowers than on their cars."

Alphonso laughed and looked back at him. "Did you know there are four seasons in Alaska?

Almost Winter, Winter, Still Winter and Construction?"

"You can hit a pothole in Alaska and total your car," Wiley answered.

"Hey, buddy, I've done that in Omaha!"

Robbie's ears had perked up along with Geoffrey's. She did some quick typing on her laptop.

"Listen to this," she read. "Tourist Warning: if you are considering doing some camping in Alaska in the summer, please note the following public service announcement. In Alaska tourists are advised to wear tiny bells on their clothing when hiking in bear country. Bells warn away MOST black and brown bears. But be careful because they do NOT scare Grizzly Bears. Tourists are advised to pay careful attention to the ground on and around the trails to be particularly alert for Grizzly Bear droppings. One can easily spot a Grizzly Bear dropping because it has tiny bells in it."

Everyone but Marge looked at Robbie and laughed.

Silence.

"Marge," Alphonso said, "Did you say something about Alaska, too? And I think you can sit down now?"

Old people! Marge stayed standing.

"Honey," Hadley said, looking at Marge, who was scowling back at her, "if you have a story, for Heaven's sake sit down. All our necks will get stiff looking at you up there."

Marge sat down.

Her knee popped again, then she held the three-page letter up and began in a firm, steady voice. "I have a distant relative who has been accused of murder."

"Oh, my," Mary Rose said.

"Say what?" Alphonso replied.

"Murder?" Hadley asked.

"That's terrible!" Robbie added.

"Excuse me!" Wiley spoke louder than he needed to. "Just how distant is this relative?"

"Yes," Mary Rose said, nodding to Wiley. "You know, Her Majesty, Queen Elizabeth, is Johnny

Depp's cousin. And that's not all that distant."

"No way!" Hadley said, turning toward Mary Rose and looking shocked.

"Way," Mary Rose said, and returned to her two down, three across crossword.

Marge rolled her eyes and took a deep breath. "My great aunt Eliza Evenbush married Hosea Hemmelfart in Wisconsin. This Alaska relative's great-grandmother was Eliza's third cousin three times removed." She took another breath.

"Their father went to Alaska to find gold after Hetzebah Hornshaw ran off with a steamboat captain headed north. Hosea also married Bertha D. Mertz and Dazee Defoliant. He had one child whom they named..."

She paused.

Silence again.

"Oh, Sweet Jesus!" Robbie groaned. She frowned at Wiley. "Why in the word did you have to ask?" She looked up at Marge, "Okay, we're ready. What horrendous name did they give this poor child?"

Marge smiled. "George," she said.

Robbie looked at Wiley and asked again, "Wiley WHY did you ask about a distant relative?"

Wiley shrugged. "I wanted to hear the outcome," he grinned. "George," he whispered to Alphonso.

"I hate to ask this," Robbie said, "but we might as well get it over with. Marge, what is your relative's name?" Robbie crouched a little in her chair, as if she was going to be hit by something other than a funny name.

"Ucksh esty ubwhask," Marge mumbled, looking down at the table.

"What?" Hadley and Alphonso said together,

"She has a Latin name?" Mary Rose asked. "We had to take two years of Latin in Catholic high school, but I don't think I remember any of those words."

Marge straitened up. "Her name is Elizabeth."

"Like the queen and Johnny Depp," Mary Rose said with a big smile.

"Whoa, whoa, whoa," Robbie said, holding up one hand. "That mumble did NOT have Elizabeth anywhere in it."

Silence.

Everyone looked at Marge.

Marge took another deep breath. Hadley thought her oxygen level must be really good by now. "Her name," and suddenly Marge looked at Robbie and gave her a big, playful grin, "her name is Buckshot Betsy Bushwhacker."

Except for Robbie, there was a soft burst of applause, every mouth at the two tables broke into grins as big as Marge's and every eye was turned to Robbie, who could not stand funny names.

Robbie looked at Marge, her mouth dropping open. "Buckshot Betsy Bushwhacker?" Robbie asked, her voice squeaky and high-pitched. "This is a joke, right?"

Marge shook her head and kept on grinning.

"Buckshot Betsy Bushwhacker," Alphonso said softly. "Has a nice ring to it." He looked at Wiley who nodded in agreement. Hadley, Mary Rose and Marge were still watching Robbie.

Robbie looked at each one of them separately. "I said it before and I'll say it again, SWEET JESUS!"

"I love it when she gets religious," Mary Rose laughed, accidentally deleting two puzzle words in the process.

Robbie slowly closed her laptop and looked serious. "Tell us about it, Marge."

Geoffrey had gone back to sleep. His "Go" had gone.

"Buckshot - we call her "Buckshot," Marge said. Robbie did the eye roll this time.

"Has a little cabin deep in the woods outside of Gospel Bird, Alaska."

"Wait a minute, wait a minute," Hadley interrupted, waving both hands in the air. "Gospel Bird, Alaska?"

"There are a lot of funny names for towns in Alaska," Robbie explained, turning on her usual scholar's mode.

"I always liked Chicken, Alaska, and there is Dead Horse, Alaska. You can't beat that one." They groaned. "The name says it all," Robbie went on.

"Just a minute," Wiley broke in," I had a Korean War buddy who lived in Kake, Alaska and his wife was from Krik, Alaska - that's K.R.I.K, not C.R.E.E.K that some people call a crick." He nodded as if pleased with himself.

Hadley stood up now, looking official. "May I nominate Manley Hot Springs, Alaska?" She smiled. "I remember a headline in an Iowa newspaper about a couple from two towns, Manley and Fertile, whose wedding announcement was in the paper, and the headline read, 'Manley man marries Fertile woman.'"

"That's the way it should be," Wiley said.

Marge was quiet, trying to look stern, but knowing her friends were coming around to where she wanted them; making plans for a long road trip.

"I had a teacher from Mary's Igloo, Alaska," Mary Rose volunteered. She didn't want to be left out.

"There's Nightmute, too," Wiley added.

They were smiling and laughing.

"And let us all remember," Robbie said in an authoritative voice. "There really is a North Pole, Alaska, just outside of Fairbanks."

They nodded and chuckled.

It doesn't take much to amuse the elderly.

"Gospel Bird has to head the list of funny names for towns," Hadley said.

Alphonso lifted one big arm. "I know what Gospel Bird means."

They were all quiet.

They looked at him.

"In my communities - the black communities- it is the custom after church service on Sunday for a church family to take the minister's family home, not for lunch mind you, but for what is still called Sunday Dinner, and at every one of those Sunday Dinners, we served fried chicken, which we called..." he paused, held his hands out palms up, and everyone at both tables replied,

"Gospel Bird!"

"Amen!" Alphonso said loudly.

"We did that at our church, too," Mary Rose said. "But when we had the priest over we just had plain fried chicken."

“White people are much less creative,” Alphonso said.

Wiley smiled and reached over to pat Mary Rose’s arm.

They were silent again.

Finally, Alphonso spoke once more, this time tenderly, his voice full of care and concern.

“Tell us about it, Marge. We may all want to go to Alaska after all.”

Marge, taking one more deep breath, began.

The Tragic Story of Buckshot Betsy Bushwhacker, Mountain Woman and the Even More Tragic Story of PickAxe Pete, Rejected Lover

"Buckshot is a big woman," Marge said. "I haven't seen her for at least twenty years, but I remember her as being a good six feet plus with big bones."

Marge, herself, was nearly that tall and she was big, too. They had no trouble imagining Buckshot's size.

"She's a real mountain woman," Marge continued. "She actually built her own log cabin along with a rather cute outhouse. I've seen a picture, I've never been there," Marge looked around to see if they needed further explanation of a "cute outhouse."

They didn't.

"She braided a rug one winter, got all her bedding from L.L.. Bean, which included queen sized sleeping bags, made an old-fashioned feather tick mattress from feathers of turkeys and birds she shot and ate, found old chairs and a couple of tables in the Gospel Bird dump when she went to town to stock up with supplies for the winter, and repaired and painted them. She painted her own pictures to hang on the walls and one entire wall is a huge fireplace bordered with shelves and shelves of books."

"Of course," Hadley said, "she chopped her own wood."

Marge nodded.

Of course.

"She only goes into town like three or four times a year when she really needs something, then she gets food and equipment that will last for months and months. She drives a 1956 Ford F100 pickup that she also found at the dump.

She paid the guy who owns the local gas station five dollars and 30 pounds of antelope meat to tow it up the mountain to her cabin, then she fixed it up and painted it. I've seen pictures of it, too, and it's a classic beauty."

"Pictures taken of it parked by the outhouse, no doubt," Wiley added. He thought for a second. "I'd like to have a 1956 Ford 100 myself."

Alphonso nodded in agreement.

"And who took these pictures?" Robbie asked. "There is not great cell phone reception in the Alaskan mountains, so I doubt she uses a smart phone. Old time Brownie camera?"

"I'll get to that part," Marge said. "The man who took the pictures also took some of Buckshot au naturel. Naked as a blue jay, in other words." She looked around at her friends, "He wasn't a bad photographer either." Alphonso and Wiley smiled.

"Buckshot must be pretty well-rounded," Wiley said.

Mary Rose reached over and hit him on the arm. She had given up on her crossword.

"So, we have a tough mountain woman who is pretty much a recluse, fends for herself, kills her own meat, I assume," Robbie said. She had pulled a map of Alaska up on her laptop and found Gospel Bird, located several miles west of Denali National Park.

"Yep," Marge nodded. "She kills her own meat and as you probably have already figured out, the girl is a crack shot. I'm good, but she could be a sniper in any armed conflict in the world. She wasn't given the name, 'Buckshot,' she earned it."

The girls didn't know if they liked Buckshot Betsy Bushwhacker or not. Alphonso definitely did. Wiley had doubts, and Geoffrey didn't care.

"So, whom did she murder?" Mary Rose asked, looking intently at Marge. Mary Rose McGill loved mysteries and everything cop-ly. She had once, years ago, visited a man in prison and from the information she pried from him, found a hidden microchip in a gangster's mansion. (***BOOB Girls II***).

"Well," Marge paused and leaned back in her chair. Her red cane swung a little from its resting spot hooked over the back. "It's 'allegedly' murdered, but you know that, Mary Rose. Let's just say the story is that," and here Marge paused, reached over and picked up the long letter that still lay on the table. She began to read:

So dear distant cousin, here's what happened. I'll just tell it like it is. Or was.

I was all alone in my cabin with the door locked really good when PickAxe Pete started knocking on the door.

"Whoa again," Robbie said. "Who was knocking at the door?"

Mary Rose leaned over toward Robbie and whispered, "I think she said Pick Ass Pete."

Wiley grinned. "Pick AXE, honey, not Pick ASS."

"Oh. Sorry." Mary Rose said, still whispering.

Wiley looked at Alphonso and began to sing the old song, "I hear ya knockin' but you can't come in."

Alphonso picked up with his deep voice. "I've got my nighty on that's oh, so thin."

The image of Alphonso in a thin nighty caused Robbie's head to drop onto her computer.

Marge gave them a stern look. "This is serious, people!" Then she thought of Alphonso in a thin, sheer nighty and started to laugh. She put the letter down, stood up, her knee popping again, walked over to him and gave him a big, wet kiss on top of his bald head.

"Okay," Alphonso said. "I like that part but continue on Detective Aaron."

Marge picked the letter up and began to read again:

As you have probably heard from sources who don't always tell the truth, PickAxe and I had an ongoing sex and love affair for some years now. Well, to be honest, since we were thirteen years old."

“Thirteen!” they all said together.

Marge did an eye roll again and took what must have been her tenth deep breath. She had sat down with a thud after kissing Alphonso. Her cane was still swinging from its hanging place and Geoffrey had moved around to be able to touch all their feet again.

PickAxe don’t like it when I lock him out, Marge read, *and he was madder than a moose in a downhill ditch. He had shot the lock off the door three or four times before and I figured he’d try that again, so I got Bear Killer loaded up and ready.*

“Her Bear Killer is an antique 1892 Saddle Ring Carbine that she restored and polished it so bright you could use it for a make-up mirror, which maybe she did as far as I know, that is, if she ever wore makeup.” Marge smiled and looked at them. They nodded in approval.

“I bet she didn’t find THAT gun in the dump,” Mary Rose said, nodding wisely.

Marge started to answer, closed her mouth, shook her head a little and went back to the letter.
So, I aimed the Bear Killer at the door and I yelled,

so he could hear me, "PickAxe Pete you git yourself outta here!"

Well he just laughs and says, "Buckshot, I ain't goin' nowhere. You know I only shoot this lock off because I love you and this lock shootin' proves it."

Now that may or may not be the case, Cousin, but I could tell he was mad as that moose in a ditch for sure, and I wasn't gonna let him bust into my cabin and try hittin' on me. He'd tried it before.

First time he tried to hit me, I broke two of his ribs - just lucky that time. Next time I slammed his nose into the back of his head and ended up cleanin' up a bucket of blood and he turned out lookin' even uglier than he was before. This time I figured all I had left was to shoot him in the balls and that would ruin a lot of things - for me as well as for him. I thought about aimin' for a knee, too, but then he'd have to stay with me and I'd have to take care of him. As you can see, there wasn't a lot of options for me here.

"Obviously a quick thinker," Hadley broke in.

"Takes in all the angles," Alphonso added.

"Is she really writing like that?" Robbie asked, "as in'cleanin' up and lookin' uglier?"

"I think she starts writing like she's thinking when she gets excited," Marge answered. She shrugged. "Danged if I know."

It made sense to Robinson Leary. Danged if she knew, either.

Marge went on: *So, I figured the best thing to do was to scare the old dude and make him go away. I figured he was bendin'over eyein' the lock, gettin' ready to put a bullet through the thing, So I take careful aim way high up on the door so as to miss him, - it would be hard to miss an entire door, you know, and like I say, I aimed high 'cause I was pretty sure he was bendin' over.*

You should have heard the door splinter and blow apart when Bear Killer fired. Blew good wood all over the place. Lock stayed on, though. It was a high-priced lock 'cause a girl can't be too careful bein' alone in the woods and all.

Once the shot quit echoin,' and my ears cleared up, there was this kind of spooky quiet.

"PickAxe?" I say, "Hey, you old son of a muskrat, say somethin'."

But PickAxe didn't say nothing.

I moved out to the door and there he was. His stupid head blown 'bout clean off. I didn't have to ask him if he was hurt or if he was okay or if he was playin'. He weren't playin.' He was dead as a volcano rock on a cool Sunday.

Then I look down at his feet, 'cause I know I shot high enough to miss his head, even if he weren't bendin' over. And guess what I saw! That vain old bucket of bull droppings was wearing boots with HIGH HEELS AND LIFTS! He was a good two or three inches higher than he shoulda been. I woulda hit him even if he was bendin' over like I thought it was.

And those boots! They was so high in the heel they looked like they belonged to that rock band with the white faces and funny black paint around their eyes - all zig zags and stuff.

"KISS!" Robbie, Marge, Hadley and Alphonso said together.

Mary Rose and Wiley looked at each other, raised their eyebrows and shrugged.

Marge sighed and looked around. She had a rapt audience. Their mouths were open. Their eyes were wide.

And four out of six knew who KISS was.

"Here's the zinger," Marge said, adjusting her glasses and looking back at the letter.

Thing is, and the reason I need your help, Cousin, is that when I loaded his body into the pickup - and it wasn't no easy thing to do, gettin' him in there, I'll tell you, and when I drove old PickAxe into town, I just took him to the undertaker's. The undertaker, Digger O'Keefe, comes a-hurryin' out and, as he looks in my driver's side window to ask why I was in his driveway, he sees old PickAxe laying there with half his head still in my yard.

Digger says, "Buckshot, what the hell did you do?"

"Shot him through the door," I say.

"Wait a minute," Hadley said, lifting her arm like a schoolgirl wanting to give the answer. "She shot him through the door. That's worse than being tasered through the balls." She pointed to Robbie.

"Worse than being knifed through the back," Robbie said, and she pointed to Mary Rose.

"Worse than being bopped in the Yazoo," Mary

Rose said without hesitating a minute. She pointed to Wiley.

Silence.

Wiley shrugged and grinned. "I got nothing," he said.

"Okay," Marge said. "This is serious. And she began to read again.

Then with all the bad luck in the world, who comes strollin' down from his sit-on-his-ass office, but the Gospel Bird Sheriff, Manley Malaprop. You'll remember him. He's Madeline Malaprop's grandson. Not even dry behind the ears and wearin' his Sheriff suit all pressed and dressed. Smartass. Ignoramus. Too little for his badge and too big his britches.

"Manley and Madeline Malaprop," Robbie mumbled. "Almost normal."

Marge glanced at Robbie and continued.

Manley looks in at old PickAxe, sees what was his face and loses his cookies all over Digger's driveway. That don't make Digger happy at all! And maybe I would have been all right if I hadn't started laughin'.

So, the moron sheriff wipes his mouth with his sleeve and says to me, "Buckshot Betsy Bushwhacker, you are under arrest for the cold-blooded murder of PickAxe Pete here. What's his last name?"

I look at Digger and Digger, he looks back at me, and we both shrug. I knew what his last name was when we was thirteen, but that was too long ago for my poor memory. Nobody remembers PickAxe's last name or his real name, either, for all it's worth.

Then Digger laughs, too, and Manley's face gets red and he gets real mad and says, "I ought to slap you both in jail. Digger O'Keefe, you just insulted an officer of the law!"

Now that I think about it, I think Digger and me, we should have done a citizen's arrest of Manley Malaprop for impersonating an officer of the law.

"So, she's in jail now?" Hadley asked. "Does she need bail?"

"I don't know about bail," Marge answered. "But she is in jail. Listen to this," and she began to read again.

So here I am in the slammer, like they call it. Manley, he has a television by his desk and I can watch that when he does, which is about all day. I think he ought to watch Andy Griffith and his sheriff show about being sheriff in Mayberry. Manley sure ain't anything like Andy Griffith. But Manley's momma, Millicent Malaprop,...

Robbie pretended to faint.

They laughed, and Marge continued.

Millicent cooks for the jail and she's a real good cook. I like eatin' here. It sure is like they say, "three hots and a cot," but Millicent has a kind heart and she brings me paper and pens and she even carried in a nice old rocking chair with a cushion and all. She had to carry it three blocks, too. Old Manley wouldn't raise a finger to help his momma. He's that kind of jerk.

So, I got to cool my heels here with Manley and Millicent until the judge comes in a couple of months from now. The judge is Judge Judge Jonkers. And that is his first name, for real - Judge. His daddy wanted him to be a lawyer, so he named him "Judge" Then when he went and did a trial, everybody would look at him and say, "What do you think, Judge?" His Daddy didn't think he'd ever be a judge, I guess, and now they have to say, "What do you think, Judge Judge?" The only problem is, he's real nice but ain't got much sense.

One time he got lost on his way to Gospel Bird and ended up 300 miles away in Haines. I don't know how he did it. There's only one road.

"Judge Judge," Robbie said softly. "I should have seen it coming, shouldn't I?"

They nodded.

Underneath the table Geoffrey yawned and farted agreement.

"How does she finish the letter, Marge?" Hadley asked.

Marge cleared her throat and read the last paragraph.

So, I hope you can come to Gospel Bird and help me. There's only one lawyer in town and he does a whole lot of nothin', except play prosecutor when the judge needs one. If you know a lawyer, bring him along. There used to be three lawyers in a firm here, Ditcher, Quick and Hyde, but Ditcher and Hyde went missing. They finished up a big case, went to Las Vegas to celebrate and were never heard of again. Some folks say they're in Mexico, but who knows? The only one left is Telfonda Quick and I'm gonna be stuck with a legal eagle prosecutor everybody calls," Slik Quick." And Slik is quick all right! And downright sneaky.

Writing with all kinds of hope,
Buckshot

“She didn’t mean to kill poor PickAss,” Mary Rose said.

“PickAxe, Honey,” Wiley said. Then he looked at Alphonso. “She’s innocent!” And he began to sing. “I didn’t KNOW the gun was loaded.”

Alphonso sang the next line, “I didn’t KNOW it, my friends.”

Together they finished, “I didn’t KNOW the gun was loaded, And I’ll never, never do it again,”

Robbie looked up from her laptop, “Don’t git no better,” she said. “Let’s go to Alaska.”

The trees around Meadow Lakes Retirement Community had just woken up from the winter. They were beginning to unfurl their leaves and the blooming trees were ready to burst into color. Every season in Nebraska has charm and beauty, but Spring - when the grass is as green as emeralds and beautiful crab apples line boulevards- that is the time when everyone takes a deep breath and says goodbye to the pure white snows of winter and the mountains of dirty snow piled into parking lots.

“Good time to go to Alaska,” Wiley said to Alphonso as they walked down the hall toward Alphonso’s office.

“If we don’t get snowed in somewhere around the high country,” Alphonso said. His scooter was chugging along beside Wiley. The old football player had slowed down, but he wasn’t down and out by any means. They knew they would take Alphonso’s customized van and outfit it for what, Wiley was sure, would be extremely comfortable sleeping. The girls would be in their Hummer, pulling their trailer. They would be a mini-caravan.

Zed Zonker, a resident of the retirement community, came strutting down the hall toward them.

Wiley didn’t like Zed and Zed didn’t like Wiley. A couple of years ago, Wiley had let the Meadow Lakes chickens loose from their classy pen on the side yard and somehow got them to chase Zonker, who had, in short time, been treed by a rooster. Zed had also once run naked, in other words he streaked, the dining room during mealtime wearing only his shoes, socks and a top hat. He swung his cane as he ran and the combination of swinging cane and swinging private parts had almost won Zed an award. If the ladies' flower show had been in full swing as well, he would have gotten the ribbon for 'best dried arrangement.' That little trick had cost Wiley three hundred dollars slapped into Zed's palm and turned out even better than either of them expected.

"Well, Vondra and Greatwood," Zed said, pointing his cane at Wiley's chest, "I hear the Washington Redskins are changing their name so they won't offend anyone." An evil grin lit up his homely face.

"Oh yeah?" Alphonso said. Being and old pro football player he knew something weird was coming.

"Yep," Zed replied, "they're dropping the name 'Washington.'"

Wiley and Alphonso groaned and walked on.

When Zed was safely behind them, Wiley turned and gave him the finger.

"That was adolescent," Alphonso said.

"It was," Wiley replied, and he grinned his own wide, wicked grin.

Part Two

The Girls, the Guys and the Dog

From *The BOOB Girls: The Musical:* The girls have met at table 12 and become close friends. They know at once that - -

Now is the Time to Talk

Now is the time to make new friends,
to talk of many things,
To open more than a book,
to share my life again.

Now is the time to be myself
with friends who can be real,
To share a laugh, to share in the fun,
to take stock. Maybe life isn't done.

Now is the time, now is the time,
now is the time to talk.

To talk of bodies that keep heading south,
of lessons life has taught,
of dreams we had in our youth,
of who we think is hot.
Now is the time to talk of what

we can do with our hair,
of whether we will even care.

About all the fears we hide,
about what is deep inside,
Now is the time to talk.

Now is the time, let's try some art,
photography and dance,
Not worried much if people stare
or look at us askance.

Now is the time for Sunday strolls
and picnics in the park,
To try new foods, explore a new path
until the people gawk.

Now is the time, now is the time,
now is the time to talk.

Now is the time to talk of sleeping alone every
night, of what goes through my mind,
Of whether it's time for romance,
of things I've never tried.

Time to talk of choices we still have to face,
of changes we've embraced,
Of how we got through it all and how to keep
standing tall.

Now is the time to talk.

The Burned Out Old Broads at Table 12, named nine years ago by a skinny, feisty, retired Sandhills rancher with what she called, "wash and wear hair."

Maggie Patten had put five shots into her mean-talking, mean-spirited, just plain mean husband's gravestone, taught them how to drive a Hummer pulling a trailer, and then had died quietly and fuss-free during a first-class storm on a cruise down the waters of the west coast.

The girls strapped her luggage around her and gave her an illegal burial at sea.

A grand idea. Never underestimate a burned out old broad.

They had loved Maggie.

She had gotten the Hummer and trailer from her brother's barn and the big Hummer H1 had been their vehicle of choice ever after. Hadley had given her big Cadillac to a granddaughter, Marge had delivered her Smart Car to a daughter, Mary Rose had done the same - given her little Chevy sedan to a granddaughter and Robbie had sold her Volvo to another professor.

Now the Hummer was nine years old. In honor of its service and good works, Hadley had treated the behemoth to new tires and a detailed cleaning in preparation for it becoming dirtier than ever before on the Alaskan trip.

Lucky HUV.

After Maggie died, her chair at Table 12 didn't stay empty for long. Calamity Doodles, a spy, had finally found a hidden microchip and earned their love. After Calamity ran off with one of the BOOB Boys (Burned Out Old Bastards) and joined the circus, Esmeralda St. Benedict had occupied the chair. Esmeralda had taken them to Fort Robinson in outstate Nebraska. There, the beautiful gypsy sorceress led them to dream themselves back into the history of the fort and find parts of their souls.

Just as the famous Crazy Horse had died at Ft. Robinson, the BOOB Girls had learned more about how to live.

Then, Marge Aaron, retired homicide detective had arrived....and stayed.

The four BOOB Girls at Table 12 loved each other, took care of each other and were totally comfortable together.

It was all about the friendship of women.

Hadley Joy Morris-Whitfield left table 12 after the Alaska decision and walked slowly down the long hallway. When she got to her large, second floor apartment, she went straight into her big, walk-in closet and stood, her hands on her hips, eying the pantsuits and outfits hanging on both sides. At the end of the closet was a large set of shelves that held shoes from floor to ceiling.

Hadley was a replacement child. A sister died nearly twenty years before Hadley was born, and her mother had always been afraid to love her. Luckily for Hadley, her father had been a pretty good mother, and even though there were times she was very afraid during her growing up, she came out of it full of graciousness and style.

She had aged well these last nine years since the girls met at table 12. She had gained only five pounds, and with the food at the retirement community, trips to Marks Bistro and Ted and Wally's Ice Cream, that was an achievement. She was a cancer survivor and, in the last couple of years, some pesky and painful arthritis started creeping into the joint of one hip.

Growing old sucks.

Hadley was tall, stately and had more money than God. She had married well, liked big men, big cars and big dogs. She had an impressive collection of pantsuits and jeans and had been a professional volunteer and socialite. At one time in her early marriage, she had even done some modeling. That ended pounds ago, but she was still slender and what some would call, “a handsome woman,” and one who knew how to apply makeup.

Her husband, not always the most faithful, had loved her and shown her off as if she were a young trophy wife. He had died when his private plane that he was piloting crashed into the side of a mountain. She had one son who had gone through three wives and was still with number four. Hadley always said the unhealthiest and most dangerous thing he ever ate was wedding cake.

A few years after her husband died, Hadley had loved an Indian sheriff, Wes Longbow, who had died two years ago. She missed Wes. She missed her husband, too, for that matter. But that was just life and she was aware that with every day, all of us on earth are one day closer to our own death. She never took anything for granted anymore and every day, as she walked down the long hall at Meadow Lakes Retirement Community on her way to the dining room and her friends, she whispered a mantra to herself:

Ever this day, I resolve
To find bits of happiness
To laugh
To recognize joy and beauty
And to live a life of gratitude
for I am a lucky, happy woman.

Once, when she hadn't said it for a long time, she was afraid she had forgotten it. She had carefully written it on the back page of her journal and she still said it almost every day.

She was indeed, a lucky, happy woman.

No one goes through life always happy. There are ups and downs. Most people describe life as a roller coaster, but Hadley liked the idea of the spinning barrel they used to have at carnivals when she was growing up. You were strapped to the inside of the barrel, standing up. It began to spin. It spun faster and faster, then the floor dropped off and centrifugal force held you against the wall, tight in your straps. When it was over, you staggered outside and threw up.

Yep. Life was like the Barrel Spin.

Robinson Leary, named for the famous black baseball player who spent a career chasing racism around the bases, was a retired professor of English from Creighton University in Omaha. After they talked some about Alaska, she left table 12, her trusty laptop under her arm. She had loved her old Toshiba, but it had died during the winter and now she carried a new HP that she had come to love as well. The girls had a surrogate son named Ken David David, and he had effortlessly moved all her information from the old computer to the new one and taught her some neat techie tricks. He was on call for her and that gave her comfort.

Old people who have computers need a Ken David David. That, or a twelve-year old.

Either one will do.

Of all the friends, Robbie was perhaps the most appreciative and grateful person. She was afraid she would outlive her money, and, because of that, she made the most of every day.

Her unlocked door opened silently, and Robinson went inside. Her parents had never locked their doors in their neighborhood of all black residents, and she felt totally safe at Meadow Lakes, even though, just a couple of years ago, the evil Dr. Fell had slipped in at night and cut a large swag out of her already short hair. Dr. Fell was trying to kill Willie Winkie, who had created a line of nightwear for senior women called, "Winkies," and he would have been happy to do away with all the girls as well.

It hadn't stopped Robbie from leaving her door unlocked.

"If someone breaks into my apartment and starts looking for money, I'll get up and help him look," she had told Hadley one evening as she watched her friend lock her door behind them.

Robinson Leary's hair had gone from salt and pepper to almost all white in the nine years she had been at Meadow Lakes. She was slender and almost as tall as Hadley. Her husband had died spooned in her arms in their bed in their Old Market apartment. He had been a professor as well, and she had loved their big table that had been stacked with books and papers and where they had worked side-by-side. Robbie had needed a change right after his death.

She retired early and moved to the retirement community where she had found table 12. She also found a romance with an Apache Indian named Raven. He was big, strong, tall, handsome and intelligent. Like Janet Evanovich's "Ranger" character, he owned a security company, but Raven made Ranger look like a short wimp. Raven had been a pro football player when Alphonso Greatwood was a Kansas City Chief linebacker. Alphonso had called in his old football buddy when Meadow Lakes had fallen victim to Dr. Fell.

Robbie thought about all that now and then.

She thought a lot more about Raven.... a lot more.

Her skin was the shade of a rich latte and she claimed both African-American heritage and a little Cajun as well. She was a descendant of the famous voodoo queen of New Orleans, Marie Laveau, but that was Robbie's secret, as was her strange ability to know who was calling when the phone rang and other things that would have come in handy at Halloween if Robbie had chosen to use them.

Robbie grabbed a diet soda out of the refrigerator and went to her little glass desk where she kept her computer and office supplies. It was a long way from the big table in the Old Market apartment. Her neighbor, Ruthie, would tell her the diet soda was bad for her, but Robbie believed that at her age she needed all the preservatives she could get.

She took a long, refreshing sip and put her computer on the desk. Robbie would be the one to make a list of all they needed to take with them. She already had the list from when they first started adventuring in the Hummer and trailer. She just tweaked it every time they hitched up.

Robbie didn't particularly like lists. She believed, as did Mark, a friend who was head of Psychology at Creighton, that lists were a way we needed to make us feel in control. She was somewhat of a control freak and she didn't like that.

She thought of a poem by her favorite poet, Edna St Vincent Millay and she said the last stanza out loud as she hooked up her computer:

My heart is warm with friends I make,
And better friends I'll not be knowing.
Yet there isn't a train I wouldn't take,
No matter where it's going.

Robbie laughed to herself and changed the word, "train" to "an RV" and repeated it.

Robinson Leary was a heart patient and she knew what her cardiologist would say when he learned she would be gone for at least two months and in a small town in Alaska. Known lovingly as "Dr. Hottie," he would look sternly at her and say, "But what about your health care?"

And Robbie would pat his knee and say, "They have these things called doctors and hospitals all over the country - even in Alaska." She had already decided to avoid the issue by not telling him.

Sometimes what doctors don't know doesn't hurt you.

Mary Rose McGill walked down the hall after they left table 12 with Marge Aaron, Geoffrey sauntering along at Mary Rose's side. He was thinking of ice cream and the thoughts were pleasant.

"We might as well do it now, Marge."

"I was thinking the same thing."

"They may not like it."

Marge looked around and behind them, as if she were checking to see if they were being followed.

Geoffrey looked around, too.

"They'll say it's too early, too soon, that we'll just have to do it over again."

"We're only in trouble if they don't notice, then we haven't done our job," Mary Rose sighed.

"We'll do the job, even if nobody else cares. We care!"

Their wicked plan was to clean the trailer like nobody's business!

"Cleanliness is next to godliness," Mary Rose finished.

Marge nodded.

The bowl of ice cream in Geoffrey's head grew bigger.

Mary Rose McGill, a sweet Catholic girl, had grown up with an alcoholic Irish father. She was sixteen when, one afternoon, at a time that found her mother out of the house, her father came at her to sexually abuse her. Mary Rose's oldest bother crashed through her bedroom door, beat the old man unconscious and pounded a note into his chest that read, "If you ever touch her again, I'll come back and kill you."

Her brother had left with his duffel bag over his shoulder, a second pair of high top tennis shoes tied around a duffel strap, and she had never seen him again. He saved her, and she never got to thank him. But her father heard the warning, and sometimes Mary Rose saw him acting as if her brother might appear to actually kill him.

Sometimes Mary Rose wished her brother actually would.

Mary Rose had four daughters. Each of them had "Mary" as her first name. "What can I say?" Mary Rose told people. "I'm Catholic!"

After their father died, Mary Rose's girls had moved their mother into Meadow Lakes without even asking if she wanted to go. She was overweight and dowdy with fourteen housedresses and two pairs of ugly shoes. But after being at table 12, with three other women who saw her as she COULD be and related to her as she could be, Mary Rose lost weight, tossed her dresses down the garbage shoot, went to Target with the girls and came away with a new wardrobe.

Peyton Claireborne, Omaha's best hairdresser, styled her hair, dyed it blonde and she ended up wearing red rimmed glasses, all because of the friendship of women.

It was Mary Rose who always said;

“Older women are beautiful!
Just look at us! Our faces are sculpted and
chiseled by joy and sorrow, tears and laughter.
Our hair is blown thin by winds of experience,
and there is so much knowledge and wisdom
in our heads, our heads can’t hold it all.
It has to trickle down through
the rest of our bodies,
and that’s why we get thicker as we age.””

She had also gotten the girls to say into their mirror every day, “I feel pretty.”

She believed “pretty” was a word older woman had let get away from them, and older women are pretty.

Her husband would be scared to death of this new, confident and pretty Mary Rose McGill, but Wiley Vondra wasn’t. Ever since the girls had sneaked into the laundry room at midnight to see if there really was a naked man there, Mary Rose had loved the man they found. It wasn’t because Wiley had, indeed, been naked, it was that he listened, respected her, teased and adored her and most of all, he loved her very much.

When Mary Rose had breast cancer, Wiley had held her at night while she cried and once he had cried with her. When Mary Rose got angry because Wiley wanted to eat the chickens Meadow Lakes had adopted, Wiley took the brunt of her Irish ire and joked with her. As he often told her, "We only get in trouble when we take ourselves too seriously."

Smart guy, that Wiley Vondra.

Marge Aaron, retired homicide detective, had been a homeless teenager. She had spent weeks sleeping under the back stoop of the beautiful old Blackstone Hotel in Omaha. During the day, she got food left by diners on tables in the elegant Gold Room, picked up soap, toilet paper and shampoo from cleaning carts in the hall and all during that time, went to school - now and then.

When she was arrested for stealing food (she called it surviving) from a little store near the hotel, the only phone number she had in her backpack belonged to an aunt she had never met. But the aunt took her in, sent her to school without the school system being able to figure out which grade she was in, and when Margie took what would now be the SAT test, she skyrocketed into fame and the police academy with more street smarts than most veteran officers.

"Marge Aaron - say it fast and it's Margarine," she had told the other three friends when they first met. She had come to Meadow Lakes on contract with the Omaha Police Department to solve the murder of one Percolator Rasmussen. The back of Perky's head had been smashed in, his throat cut, a nylon cord twisted around his neck, a bullet hole in his jacket and a knife in his back. It didn't take Marge long to figure out this was probably not a suicide.

What a cop!

Marge was a large lady who should be large. She would have looked strange thin and petite. She liked to say that a recent study showed that women who were somewhat overweight tended to live longer than men who mentioned it.

Her knees were bad (one had been replaced) and she was stiff as a rail when she got up in the morning. "Old age is coming at a really bad time," she said now and then.

She had been a good cop, solved some bad murders and put away some bad guys. Her colleagues had respected her and she was proud of that and proud that she had married law enforcement and given birth to law enforcement. Her husband was a "cop's cop" and her children were police and FBI.

And Marge had good street sources. Once, right after her knee replacement, she came out of the shower, put on her elastic knee brace and caught her ring in the fabric on the inside of the brace. She couldn't get her hand out no matter what she did.

She wiggled and limped to her phone, called Omaha's leading breaking and entering burglar, and told him what had happened. Within minutes he was through three locks on her door, pouring himself a cup of coffee in the kitchen and grinning from ear to hear. Without saying a word, he took out a switchblade, cut off the brace, kissed the top of Marge's head and left - still grinning and still sipping coffee from her favorite mug.

What a cop, indeed!

The Red Cane

Marge's prize procession was a lethal weapon; a red cane, shiny and bright. It was usually at home hung casually over the back of whatever chair was holding her ample behind.

The cane seemed to have a personality of its own and it had "bling". Push one jewel and it turned into a taser, another and it was a low-powered rifle, a third jewel sent tripping pellets all over the floor and a fourth produced a huge smoke screen. The final jewel shot knives out the sides and there was a golden lariat in the handle, just like Wonder Woman's.

Wonder Woman was such a comic book superhero, especially to the young Marge who had always carried three beat-up Wonder Woman comic books in her back pack when she lived on the streets.

Marge loved her red cane, and for that matter, so did the other BOOB Girls.

It tended to come in handy now and then.

The BOOB Girls: warrior women of justice!

BOOB Girls: Wear it with Pride!

Their motto was Never Underestimate A Burned Out Old Broad.

Geoffrey the Mastiff was an oversized representative of the noble breed. His records, retrieved from the evil Busch family who purchased Meadow lake five years ago, before Alphonso took over, showed his mother to be a Fila Brasileiro, the largest mastiff breed. His father, uncertain and unknown, was thought to have been an oversized Bull Mastiff.

Romantic stranger!

While the Fila Mastiff has a mean temperament, an ugly personality and is dangerous, Geoffrey, all 175 pounds of him, took all his love from his daddy and was nothing but a pussycat and lover. He was, indeed, many things, including excitable, energetic, awkward, loyal, fun-loving and friendly with a keen desire to protect his ladies and be their lap dog. Point to a bad man and yell PLAY and Geoffrey was in the air and the bad guy was on the ground,

Like the girls, Geoffrey was growing older. His right back leg had some arthritis and he slept more than usual, which was a lot, no matter how you counted it. Geoffrey was intelligent and knew a lot of words, in addition to 'Play'. He knew go, here, come, ride, ice cream, good dog, sit (used on occasion), lay down (used more often) and the one he hated. Bad Geoffrey! He avoided that one and when he was Bad Geoffrey he didn't mean to be.

Smart puppy, Geoffrey. Good dog!

He had taken a liking to Mary Rose's make up, had licked it off when she thought he was attacking her and after he really got a taste of Estee Lauder, he never left her side, even when his legal owner, the cunning Thorny Busch called him to come. As soon as he could, he was back at Mary Rose's feet.

He was their rescuer, their footrest, their dog.

When you have a dog who loved you, you are a lucky woman indeed and these were four lucky women.

Alphonso Greatwood and Wiley Vondra were close friends. They had gone down the hall from the dining room together and met Zed Zonker. They went into Alphonso's over-priced office and relaxed. Alphonso took out two cigars and they began to talk about what they needed to do to customize Alphonso's van so they could sleep, drink and shower in it. A toilet would be helpful, too.

Some men are brilliant.

While the girls believed that women have a different friendship gene than men - making friends quicker, keeping them longer and having more, these two men were like brothers who liked each other.

Alphonso Greatwood is a big black man, who had been a linebacker for the Kansas City Chiefs when the club really got underway in the 1960's. He was still huge. Even though he wasn't terribly overweight, his big frame and his still-strong muscles had added to the body stress caused by the many hits he took on the field and his knees were shot beyond repair.

Both his knees and Marge's looked as if they had lost a head-butting contest with midgets.

Alphonso Greatwood was pretty much scooter-bound. When he did walk, it was with two large canes. But his scooter was custom made and outstanding. The Green Machine was, of course, painted green. It had a detachable roll bar and a GPS. When Alphonso pushed one button, it played the Nebraska fight song. A second button rendered the theme song from the old television show; "Happy Days," because Alphonso Greatwood was the original "Fonz." There was a seat behind the driver's that had "Bitch Seat" written on it.

Last year, when he began to gently and tenderly court Marge Aaron, he had painted the seat yellow, realized the whole scooter looked like it belonged to a Green Bay Packer, and he had repainted the seat in the same green shade as the rest of The Green Machine.

Good move.

Alphonso basked in his notoriety. He was still interviewed by sports writers. The sports broadcast team of Mike and Mike called him now and then for a commentary. When his long-time football opponent and good friend, Raven, was at Meadow Lakes, the two old pros still made an impressive entrance into the dining room.

He also basked in his love for Meadow Lakes. Reluctant to move there because a retirement community meant he was growing old, he came to love the place so much he bought it from the wicked Busch family from Florida.

Thorney, Lilac and Rose Busch had turned it into a den of iniquity with liquor, gambling, prostitution, and an underground Viagra ring.

Alphonso was a good owner. Sheryl, his manager was good, too, and together they made the place a showroom for modern retirement living and luxury.

Not to mention a heck of a lot of fun.

Wiley Vondra, a little older than Alphonso, was tall and lanky. A cowboy at one time in western Nebraska, he was always seen in cowboy boots, a brown leather vest and a Stetson hat. While each apartment had a washer and dryer, on the 15th of every month, hat, vest and boots were all Wiley wore when he did his laundry in the old Meadow Lakes laundry room where he could do a month's worth of laundry at one time.

Imagine his underwear drawer.

The girls had met him there when Maggie Patten threw open the door to the laundry room, found Wiley at a card table with a hand of solitaire and Willie Nelson wailing on a boom box.

"Hello, Ladies!" He had grinned. "You want a game of poker?" Now, he and Mary Rose were an item and had cared deeply for each other for nine years.

Wiley was a Korean War veteran, "The Forgotten

War," he called it, and he still, now and then on certain dates, wept in the shower. On other days, the song that was played over and over for the troops ran through Wiley's head and he would softly sing aloud, "Rag Mopp, Doo-doo-doo-DAH-dee ah dah. Rag Mop, Doo-doo-doo-DAH-dee ah dah. Rag Mop, R-a-g-g-m-o-p-p-Ragg Mop!." He often sang it all the way down the long hall as he went to his apartment.

Wiley had never married after he returned from the war, had no children or pets. But now he had Mary Rose McGill and considered himself a lucky man.

A very lucky man indeed.

As friends, the six of them; Hadley, Robbie, Mary Rose, Marge, Wiley and Alphonso were family. They cared for each other and there was nothing they could not say or think or feel. Their friendship was what everyone wants and needs and for which we sometimes have to search. There was nothing held inside, nothing too secret not to tell.

Feel lucky about your friends.

Part Three
On the Road

From: *The BOOB Girls: The Musical:* Leaving Meadow Lakes with no forwarding address.

On the road, on the road,
any road you want to drive.

On the road, on the road,
the maps are left behind.

Take a chance,
make a turn that's how we get through life.

On the road, on the road,
who knows when we'll arrive.

Goodbye to schedules, goodbye to phones.

We'll have each other, wherever we roam.

So long ceiling. Hello the sun.

We'll take the journey, till the journey's done.

On the road, on the road,
any road you want to drive.

On the road, on the road,
any road you want to drive.

Take a chance, make a turn,
that's how we get through life.
Take a chance, make a turn,
that's how we get through life.

On the road, on the road,
who knows when we will arrive.
On the road,
on the road who knows when we will arrive.

On the road, on the road,
any road you want to drive.
On the road, on the road,
any road you want to drive.

Spring was bursting into bloom outside the floor-to-ceiling dining room windows. Hundreds of tulips were in full bloom, bordered by edges of daffodils. Crab apple trees were competing to see which could be heavier with scented flowers, reds or whites. Lilacs were urging on their buds and the grass was thick and green. It would be a good spring.

The six friends sat around table 12, maps spread out, tablets, phones and note pads at the ready.

Geoffrey was on his back under the table, long legs in the air, bent at the knees. His head was against the coolness of Alphonso's Green Machine. He liked the feel of the metal. One ear was raised and one eye open. Whatever his people were talking about sounded good. He could tell their voices were happy, good dog voices.

Everyone was excited and filled with anticipation.

Everyone except Mary Rose McGill.

"You know," Alphonso said, "As I think about it, I've always wanted to drive the Alcan Highway. Every time I was in Alaska it was fly into Anchorage, fly out of Anchorage."

"I read about it," Robbie said, smiling, "the highway was completed in 1942 as a war highway to connect the lower states with Alaska across Canada. 1700 miles. Presently, it's 1300 some because it's under constant construction and is paved all the way, now."

"Like that one thing we heard," Wiley added, "Four seasons of Alaska: almost winter, winter, still winter and construction."

"There are all kinds of problems," Robbie put in. "There are rock slides, hoar frosts, ice, and they even have what they call 'ice heaves' where the highway buckles."

"I don't care," Wiley said. "It's my dream to go there and I'm glad we're going."

They all nodded.

Except Mary Rose McGill.

She looked up at them. "I want to go too," she stammered, "but my girls are threatening to get a restraining order or something to keep me here. One of my Mary's was crying when she said she was sure I would be eaten by a bear."

They laughed then immediately became sober again.

Robbie reached over and took hold of Mary Rose's hand. "If you and Wiley are out in the woods messing around and a bear sees you, remember, Mary Rose. You don't HAVE to outrun the bear. You just have to outrun Wiley."

They laughed.

Mary Rose laughed, too.

"What am I thinking?" She said. "I'm not even going to tell them when we're going. I'll just be quiet and we'll just be gone."

"We kidnapped Robbie when she didn't want to stay in the hospital," Hadley said. "My gosh, that was nine years ago! And since we're good at kidnapping, we can kidnap you, Mary Rose."

Mary Rose leaned forward. "You know that old song from South Pacific? Bloody Mary sings it, I think. 'You gotta have a dream, if you don't have a dream, how you gonna have a dream come true?' Well, we have a dream. And a lot of people our age have stopped dreaming. Look at the residents here who have exactly the same routine day after day after day."

They nodded, and Hadley added, "That can be comforting though. Safe."

"God preserve my big, awkward body from feeling safe all the time," Alphonso said. "Do you know how many residents are here because their doctors are in Omaha and we're near a hospital? That's living in fear, not safety."

Mary Rose stood up. "Okay. I say if any of us dies during this trip - this adventure - this lifetime dream, then we'll die doing what we want to do!"

"Hear, hear!" Alphonso said.

"That's my girl!" Wiley said, patting Mary Rose's bottom. "Actually, it hasn't been a lifetime dream for me. I only started thinking about it four days ago," He patted her bottom again and she tried to sit on his hand.

"Sounds good to me," Marge said and was surprised when Alphonso reached over, took her hand and kissed it.

"I'll drink to that," Hadley said, raising her coffee cup.

"And," Robbie said seriously, "because we all feel this way, we really do need to get our affairs in order and tell each other what we want done if - and it's not likely but IF - one of us should actually die on this trip."

"Cremate me," Alphonso said. "And I'm glad I didn't get all skinny and lean. When I'm cremated I want to start a fat fire!"

They laughed.

"Who's for cremation?" Marge asked.

Hadley, Robbie, Alphonso, and Marge raised their hands.

"Gotta put me in a cheap casket," Wiley said.

"Me, too," May Rose added. "I plan to be buried with my late husband on one side and Wiley on the other side, and I'll have them lean me a little bit toward Wiley."

She smiled at him.

He made a move for her bottom again.

"Mary Rose McGill," Hadley smiled, too. "You made a funny!"

Dream on.

They talked of many things, as Robbie would say, of cabbages and kings, but mostly of packing, places where they wanted to stop on the way, and what they wanted to see.

"The journey is part of the fun," Marge said.

They talked of clothes to take and not to take. "If you bring anything home you haven't worn, you have over packed," Hadley pronounced. With four women in a trailer, clothes had to be kept at a minimum.

"Listen to these great names," Robbie said, scrolling down on her laptop. "Dawson Creek, where the highway begins, Charlie Lake, Upper Laird, Watson Lake, Jakes Corner, Haines Junction, Tok. It's like a romance novel in and of itself."

"And don't forget Chicken, Alaska, and the great and wonderful village of Gospel Bird," Marge grinned.

"We are indeed the dreamers," Robbie closed her laptop and looked at her friends. Then, she reached out her hands and took hold of Marge's and Hadley's wrists. "How many people our age can say that?"

They smiled and nodded.

"I have a friend who brought one back from a cruise to Alaska, and I want to get an Inukshuk!" Mary Rose announced after a minute of thoughtful quiet.

Everyone except Robbie said, “Say what?”

“You find an Inukshuk,” Robinson Leary added. “Then we’ll look for ulus.”

Inukshuks? Ulus?

They grinned at each other as if they knew something none of their friends knew.

They were right.

On the Road

The night before an adventure can be interesting. They ate dinner together in a packed dining room at Meadow Lakes. Every one of them ate lighter than usual, hoping they would sleep better. Sheryl, Meadow Lakes manager, joined them for the first half hour and she and Alphonso went over what needed to be done and any special bills that had to be paid early.

They planned to be gone for two months, and that was a guess. Who knew what would happen to Buckshot Betsy Bushwhacker?

Half the people at the retirement community envied them.

The other half were relieved it wasn't them who would be driving a Hummer and a trailer to Alaska.

Hadley and Robbie walked down the hall together. Hadley smiled at Robbie. "My son insists I get a satellite phone in case we break down or need help where there is no cell phone service."

"Are you going to do it?" Robbie asked.

"Nope," Hadley said. "It's an adventure for Pete's sake."

"I also read on an Alaska web page that, 'Help is only a wave away.' Seems you have to stop and help if someone needs it."

Good idea.

They gave each other a quick hug when they got to Robbie's apartment.

"Sleep tight," she told Hadley,

"Same back atcha," Hadley smiled.

But Hadley didn't s sleep tight. None of them did. When Hadley was still awake at 3 a.m., she got up and went into her kitchen. A friend had told her that if you eat three tablespoons of peanut butter and drink a small glass of milk, you'll go right back to sleep. She ate the peanut butter then opened her refrigerator to see that she had cleaned it out and tossed the milk. She shut the refrigerator door and went back to bed.

Peanut butter alone would have to do the job.

Mary Rose and Wiley took Geoffrey outside to find a tree, then went to Wiley's apartment.

Mary Rose slept with Wiley. Actually, Mary Rose lay awake with Wiley. They talked, going over a lot of things they had talked about at dinner. Finally, they got up, wrapped up in blankets and took two glasses of wine out onto Wiley's balcony. It was a beautiful night and a few nighthawks who lived on the hospital roof across the street dived for food and sounded their mournful cries. Geoffrey debated going with them onto the balcony, but chose to stay sprawled out across the foot of the bed. It was HIS bed and they could get back in the best way they could.

Geoffrey slept soundly all night.

Robbie called Raven, the Apache, at midnight and they talked for an hour. He told her he might be able to meet them in Gospel Bird before they left the little village. Other people ran his security agency but one of the cases he was on now pretty much required him to be in different places in the lower forty-eight.

About 2a.m., Robbie sat up in bed and talked to the ragged little bear who sat on her pillow. When she pressed one paw her mother told her how proud she was of her. The other paw had a recording of her husband telling her how he loved her. The little bear would go to the Hummer tucked under Robbie's arm.

This time she held the little bear up in front of her face and, in the darkness of her bedroom, said to the bear, “Do you think I can count tossing and turning as exercise?”

The bear didn’t answer.

Alphonso lay awake until midnight as well, then used his two canes to maneuver into his kitchen where he dug into the “last minute bag” on his counter, the one that would be the last thing he took to the van. His clothes, and Wiley’s as well, had been hung up or put away in the new customized vehicle.

From the bag he pulled out a bottle of very expensive cognac and poured two fingers into a brandy glass. He took it back to his bed, holding it carefully while he moved on the canes. and sat on the bed. From his spot on the bed he could look out his big windows in his bedroom. A cat bounced across the lawn, a bird was awakened and gave a sleepy “peep,” and he watched as headlights turned the corner and went past Meadow Lakes.

His Meadow Lakes.

What would happen on this long trip?

And would they all come back and would they all be well?

Old people worries. He shook his head, took the last sip of his drink, grabbed his comforter and slid under clean, crisp sheets. He went to sleep.

Marge Aaron, the last of our heroes, watched the nine o'clock news, snuggled into her bed, began a mantra of prayers she used every night and went to sleep.

She slept soundly and peacefully until 5 a.m.

Two sound sleepers out of seven ain't bad.

At five o'clock, her phone gave her a loud text alert, "If you are all awake, let's go!" Hadley sent a text to all of them, and while they had planned to eat in the dining room when it opened at six, they were all in the parking lot, gathered around the Hummer and trailer and Alphonso's van by five thirty.

It was pitch black. There was no moon.

They had hitched the RV up to the Hummer the day before. They piled in amid laughter and joyous sounds.

Just the way travelers should start an adventure.

As they drove out the Meadow Lakes parking lot, they saw Zed Zonker waving to them from in front of the dining room door, his cane over his arm. He was silhouetted in the light behind him.

They waved back.

On the road, on the road
Any road you want to drive

They crossed the wide Missouri, looking to their left at the lights from the Robert Kerrey Pedestrian Bridge dancing in reflections on the water. They greeted Iowa and turned left onto Interstate Highway 29. The sun still wasn't up. They had a wonderfully early start.

They talked about how they would be at Mt.. Rushmore, their first stop, by late afternoon. As the first pink streak appeared in the east, they saw the sign telling them Missouri Valley, Iowa, was their next exit.

"Remember that great commercial by Chip Davis?" Hadley said.

"About C.J. McCall and the waitress named Mavis in the Old Home Fill 'er Up, Keep on A-Truckin' Café." Robbie laughed.

Mary Rose nodded in agreement. "And he had a dog named Sloan, after Sloan, Iowa, down the road."

There was a minute of silence, then Mary Rose let out a scream.

"Stop! Stop! Stop!" She yelled, each "Stop!" getting louder and more desperate.

Marge made a sharp turn onto the exit ramp leading to Missouri, Valley. "Ye Gods, Mary Rose! What's wrong?"

Mary Rose answered with one word, "Geoffrey!" They all looked at Geoffrey's usual place in the rear storage area of the Hummer.

It was empty all right.

Marge picked up her cell phone and pressed the little call button. "Call Alphonso," she said into the phone.

He answered on the first ring and Marge also had just one word, "Geoffrey."

Marge and Alphonso both drove the rest of the way up the exit ramp, turned left onto the local highway and exited back toward Omaha.

Half an hour later they drove into the circle drive in front of Meadow Lakes. Mary Rose and Wiley both threw open their doors. Wiley motioned Mary Rose to get back into the Hummer and he hurried as fast as his old legs would take him through the front door and down the hall to his apartment.

"So dumb, so dumb, so dumb!" Mary Rose kept repeating. "How could I forget him? I'm sorry, Geoffrey, I'm sorry."

"He isn't here yet, honey," Marge told her, with a tender smile.

In just minutes, Wiley and Geoffrey hurried out the front door. Geoffrey found a tree and took what seemed like a long time to sniff, pee, then sniff and pee some more. When he saw Mary Rose holding open the door on the back of the Hummer, he broke into a run, leaped into the back area, turned himself around, leaned out and licked Mary Rose's face.

"I'm so glad I remembered you, Geoff!" Mary Rose said, and she hugged his big body.

"I'm glad she remembered him before we got to Mt. Rushmore!" Marge said.

They started off again, at almost exactly the time they had planned to leave when they first talked about it.

This time, they exited again at Missouri Valley and headed into the McDonald's parking lot. Already there were several cars parked and a line at the drive through.

They parked the trailer at the far end of the parking lot. Alphonso wheeled the van into a handicap parking space, grabbed his two canes and he and Wiley met them at the door.

“This is definitely not healthy,” Robbie said.
“Hey lady,” Alphonso said, “like you say, at our age we need all the preservatives we can get.”

They all ordered egg, cheese and sausage biscuit breakfast sandwiches and enjoyed every evil bite. Just to show off, Alphonso and Wiley had an oversized order of fries.

“We’re all going to die anyway,” Hadley said.

They nodded and settled into a comfortable booth. As they ate, the day welcomed them and promised to be sunny and pleasantly warm.

Geoffrey watched out of his back window, steaming it over every time he breathed, knowing there would be something good for him coming out of this strange place with the great smells.

Mount Rushmore

They truly enjoyed the day. All the girls except Hadley, who had macular degeneration and was smart enough to know she shouldn't drive, drove the Hummer. Wiley and Alphonso switched seats as well, Alphonso falling asleep the minute he moved to the passenger side, Wiley making big adjustments in Alphonso's driver's seat.

Every hour or so, they stopped at rest stops or small towns and got out and stretched their legs, had a drink of soda, coffee, juice or water, grabbed a snack now and then from the trailer refrigerator. At every stop they let Geoffrey check out who had been there before him.

It was early and still light outside when Robbie began to check out campgrounds near Mt.. Rushmore.

"How does Horsethief Lake Campground sound?" She asked.

"I like the name," Hadley said.

"Good to me," Mary Rose added.

"Navigate," Marge said to Robbie, who

immediately instructed her smart phone to take them to the camp ground.

Mary Rose called Wiley and told him where they were headed. In less than an hour they pulled into a tree-filled, shady campground and, in less than a half hour more, they had two pull-through sites and were outside hooking up the trailer and van and setting up the inside of the trailer.

Two sewers, two electrical connections and two waters were ready to use. The trailer was homey and welcoming. The van, in one day, had turned into a respectable, mobile man cave.

As the sun began to set, there was a checkered tablecloth on the picnic table, Alphonso's portable grill was at the ready and hamburgers were stacked on a plate ready to cook.

Hadley brought out two bottles of wine, crystal wineglasses and goblets for water as well. While a lot of RVers insist on plastic glasses and dishes for every occasion, Hadley insisted on real crystal, carefully wrapped and covered when they traveled. So far, not a single glass had broken.

Elegance on a campground scale. For hamburgers.

"Crazy Horse Memorial," Robbie said as she sat down. They would visit the memorial early the next day and she gave them more details on the massive sculpture being carved in a mountain sacred to the Lakota tribes. They listened, nodded and were impressed.

"Started in 1948," Hadley said. "Think of that."

"May be the biggest mountain sculpture in the world when it's finished," Marge said.

"We won't live to see it done," Mary Rose added.

"Paha Sapa," Robbie said. "Indian for 'Black Hills.'"

Hadley was lost in thought. She remembered how Wes Longbow, the sheriff she had loved, had been at Fort Robinson and dreamed himself back in history to witness the death of Crazy Horse, great Lakota warrior. In his dream, he had held Crazy Horse's hand as he died.

"This is a good day to die," Hadley said out loud.

"That's the famous quote from Crazy Horse before the Indians attacked George Armstrong Custer," Robbie said.

"Wouldn't it be great if we could all say that as our time on earth ends?" Hadley said as Alphonso put the first hamburger on the grill. "This is a good day to die."

Geoffrey, not into philosophy, squirmed his way under the picnic table and waited for something tasty and meat-like to drop.

The New Mt. Rushmores

There they were, the four giant heads; George Washington, Thomas Jefferson, Abraham Lincoln and Theodore Roosevelt. The six friends stood on the viewing area in a crisp, cool mountain morning. Hadley's jacket was too light, and she shivered now and then.

"Impressive," Alphonso said.

They nodded.

They didn't need to be overly impressed. It was cold. They started down the sloped walkway to the visitor's center and coffee shop.

When they were half way down, Mary Rose looked at them. "SHIT!" She said, just loud enough for them to hear but too soft for people walking around them.

They knew what it meant. Shoulders back, Head high, I's (eyes) straight ahead, Tummy tucked in. The girls straightened up and, for several minutes, they had excellent posture for old ladies.

They two guys didn't care, and anyway, Alphonso always sat straight on his scooter.

The coffee shop was cozy and warm. Their jackets and Marge's red cane were all on the backs of their chairs. Wiley treated them to coffee and donuts. It felt good. They were on the road for sure now.

Geoffrey stretched out in his Hummer compartment and let visions of milk bones float through his head. He slept.

"I have an idea," Mary Rose announced.

"Oh boy," Wiley said, "this can be dangerous."

Mary Rose smiled. "Wiley and Alphonso, you create a football Mt.. Rushmore. Who would be the four best players ever who you would carve into a mountain. And we," she pointed to the girls, "will name the four greatest women athletes."

"Foul!" Alphonso said. "Yellow flag! There are four of you and two of us. You have to have TWO groups of women." He grinned. "Good luck, ladies."

"Can we put on the entire University of Nebraska's volley ball team?" Robbie asked.

Alphonso pretended to give her the evil eye.

They huddled at the table, fresh, steaming cups of coffee at the ready.

It took over half an hour, and some heated argument between the men, before Mary Rose and Wiley both had the names of their nominees entered in their smart phones.

“Okay,” Mary Rose said, pointing at Wiley. “Go. Who are the four best pro players in history?”

Wiley stood up and Alphonso straightened up. “We had a slight disagreement on number four, but I’ll explain later.” He looked at Alphonso. “The greatest football player of all time is....” The girls did a drum roll with their hands on their table.

“Jim Brown!” Alphonso said, “Running back for the Cleveland Browns. Late 1950’s to mid 60’s.”

“And the second face on our football Mt.. NFL is...” he motioned for another drum roll. He got it.

“Lawrence Taylor!” Alphonso almost yelled. “Linebacker, NY Giants, 1980’s.”

“Whoa, whoa!” Robbie exclaimed. She looked at Alphonso and Wiley. “You named Jim Brown number one and didn't double it up with Otto Graham?"

The two men looked surprised.

"Brown wouldn't have been so much that last year without Otto Everett Graham," Robbie said, sternly. "He still holds the record for passing attempts and he took the Browns to league championships and won seven of them. He is THE GREATEST quarterback in history."

She folded her arms and leaned back in her chair.

"Holy Moly!" Wiley said.

"Ye Gods!" Alphonso said.

Mary Rose leaned over toward Hadley. "Who's Otto Graham?" she asked.

"Who's Jim Brown?" Hadley whispered back.

"How do you know about Otto and Jim?" Alphonso asked.

Robbie shrugged. "My dad was a sports fanatic and grew up in Cleveland."

Enough said.

Never underestimate a burned out old broad.

She motioned for the men to continue with their wimpy selections.

Wiley nodded in approval. "And number three is…." Another drumroll.

"Johnny Unitus, Quarterback, Baltimore Colts, 1950's and 60's," Alphonso said.

"We disagreed on number four," Wiley told them. "Or number five if Otto goes in. Alphonso votes for Joe Montana, quarterback for the San Francisco 49ers. 1980's, 90's."

"Joe Cool, The Catch, Superdrive," Alphonso added.

"I disagree," Wiley said.

They waited for more. Wiley grinned, put his hand on his friend's shoulder, and was almost teary as he said, "I voted for Alphonso Greatwood, Kansas City Chief's Linebacker, 1970's."

Alphonso looked surprised when they all applauded.

"Hear, hear!" Hadley said, raising her cup.

She was toasting with coffee cups a lot lately.

There was a short silence.

Robbie stood up. "We picked the women Iditarod champions, and we admit, we had to look it up on Robbie's phone."

Wiley and Alphonso looked at each other. They had looked up their players, too.

"First woman to win the Iditarod, the greatest dogsled race in the world, Alaska's world series," Robbie was on a roll and another roll followed - the drum roll. "Libby Riddles, 1985, Then Mary Shields, 1974. She didn't win, but she was the first woman to finish,"

"Finishing is good," Wiley nodded.

"Finishing is winning in that one," Alphonso added, being as supportive as possible.

"Then we have two different poses of the really great champion," she nodded for a drum roll.

"There are only three women that we found, but the greatest is Susan Butcher. She won four out of five years in the 1980's and 90's. It was a joke that when she won for the fourth time men were crouched in corners giving themselves estrogen shots."

They laughed.

"For our next four women," Robbie sat down, and Mary Rose stood up. "First is the greatest woman athlete and arguably possibly the greatest single athlete in the world," -drum roll. - "Babe Didrikson Zaharias. She was the national Amateur Athletic Union TEAM champion and 1932 Olympic Gold Medal winner. She was the only person on our AAU team and she won every team event. In other words, Babe WAs the entire team."

Mary Rose read their last selection, "We decided on the UNL women's volleyball team. That's our story and," she pointed to Alphonso, "we're sticking to it."

Once more, they raised their coffee cups in a salute.

On day four they took a bus tour of the Little Bighorn Battlefield and as soon as they got back in the Hummer, Wiley and Alphonso insisted on playing Peter Garcia's tasteless and tacky,

"Please Mr. Custer, I don't want to go," song on You Tube. Wiley did equally tasteless and tacky war whoops.

Then, as soon as the music stopped, there was a minute of silence. They drove off, and before their wheels were outside the battlefield gate, they became serious.

"It was horrible," Mary Rose said, "what we did to the Indians."

"It was brutal all right," Wiley agreed. "It was war and America does war."

"Can you imagine thousands of buffalo rotting in the sun because the white merchants wanted coats and hats to sell in the east?" Marge asked.

Hadley was quiet. She was once again thinking of Wes Longbow holding Crazy Horse's hand.

"It was genocide," Robbie concluded. "Pure and simple."

They were quiet for the rest of the trip back to their campground.

They had been five days out when their next stop came into view, Glacier National Park.

Wiley had wanted to stop here for a day, and it sounded like a good idea. The problem was, it was raining a slow, steady, chilly rain.

Mary Rose put on her plastic, hooded raincoat and got Geoffrey in and out of the Hummer as quickly as possible when he told her he needed a tree.

Geoffrey let them know he wanted to stay outside longer by carefully waiting until he got into his back compartment, moving as close to the far back seat as possible, then shaking as hard as he could, not once, but three times. Drops of water flew onto the windows and seats. Each time whoever was sitting in the back yelled and said something intelligent, like, "Don't do that, Geoffrey!"

Geoffrey just grinned, turned around three times, lay down and went to sleep.

This was a good Big Ride.

After a day of driving through the park in the rain and oohing and awing at the scenery, they drove through the little Hungarian town of Babb, Montana. There, in a back corner off the highway was a small, almost unnoticeable café advertising the best hamburgers in the world.

"Gotta give 'em credit for their confidence," Wiley said.

They stopped.

The rustic sign on the door said simply, "The Huns Den."

"Babb, Hungarian town," Robbie observed.

They went inside to a cozy, homey little café with a window table and high stools looking out onto the mountains. There were only a few tables in a relatively small dining room. They gathered at the long table that looked out the window. Marge and Alphonso stood their canes up against the wall.

They were greeted by a young woman who pleasantly took their orders for sodas and burgers and then, almost at the same time, they were greeted by a little boy, six or seven years old. He was staring unashamedly at Alphonso.

Alphonso looked back at him and grinned.

"You're really big!" the boy said.
"I am," Alphonso said, "and I used to play football."

The little boy walked over to the big linebacker and held out his hand, "I'm Benedek."

"Alphonso," they shared a firm handshake and Alphonso pointed to each of the friends and said their names. They all said, "Hi" to Benedek who nodded and spelled his name for them.

"We're of Hungarian descent," he announced proudly. Then he looked at Alphonso again. "You want to arm wrestle? I'm good."

"Yeah, well I'm good, too," Alphonso said.

Benedek climbed up onto the high chair next to Alphonso at the long table, very seriously sat with his legs braced on the rungs and held up his arm in arm wrestling tradition.

Alphonso responded, and they began a championship arm wrestling contest.

In just seconds, Alphonso faked a fall and said, "Man! You are good!"

The group applauded.

"Two out of three!" Benedek said loudly.

Alphonso faked another fall and asked, "Where did you learn to do that?"

"It's a natural talent," Benedek beamed, and when he saw his mother coming out of the kitchen with a huge platter of giant hamburgers and baskets of French fries, he waved goodbye, scurried out a side door and disappeared into the trees.

"Neat kid," Wiley said.

"Great looking burgers," Marge announced.

They really, probably were, the best burgers in the world.

Sometimes a trip is worth the food.

As they were eating, Marge announced that she had talked to Buckshot Betsy and asked her if she needed bail, since they would be another few days on the road before they finally got to Gospel Bird.

"She wants to stay in jail," Marge said. "Manley's mother, Millicent, brought in a card table and four chairs along with treats and two friends. They sat up the table and treats in Betsy's cell and are teaching her to play Bridge. She said

Manley, and I quote Buckshot here, 'like to throwed a fit,' that his mother did that, but she gave him a good 'what for' and the Bridge lessons continue.

"They also brought her a 'real nice pilla,'" she made quote marks in the air with her fingers, looked at them, smiled and said, "Pillow. And a handmade crazy quilt for her cot. She's more comfortable than she would be in her cabin. And get this, yesterday the ladies gave her a shower with all kinds of toiletries: lotions, shampoos, soaps, body wash, face cream and cologne from Walmart. Millicent has pretty much adopted Buckshot."

"I assume the ladies of Gospel Bird were not fond of PickAxe Pete," Alphonso observed.

Never underestimate a Burned Out Old Broad.

On the Road, On the Road, The Maps are Left Behind

In another two days they were standing under the famous sign in Dawson Creek, British Columbia, Canada, that announced the beginning of the Alaska-Canada Highway, the famous Alcan.

"Just the name is romantic," Mary Rose said longingly, "Dawson Creek."

She was holding Wiley's hand in the big parking lot in front of the sign. Three other RVs were parked near their trailer and the van.

"Will you take our picture?" a young woman asked Marge. She was with a handsome young man and their SUV was obviously outfitted for tent camping.

Marge positioned them under the sign that read:

You are now entering the
World Famous
Alaska Highway
Dawson Creek, B.C.

The sign that said, "Mile 0" was nearby.

"Mile zero," Mary Rose whispered, looking at the big, colorful sign in the intersection of Dawson Creek's main street and the highway.

"Now take our picture," Marge said, smiling at the young couple. Three more campers had pulled into the Mile Zero parking lot and people from all over the world were gathering by the sign.

The young man took cameras and phones from the six friends and they stood together for the photo shoot.

"Wait a minute," Robbie said. She pulled Hadley in behind Mary Rose, who was standing beside Wiley, moved Marge three feet to the left to be beside Alphonso who was balancing on his two canes, and stood back and looked at the pose.

"Just right," she smiled.

"Excuse me," Hadley said, "are you in this picture of not?"

Robbie looked surprised, "Oh," she said, "right," and she took her place next to Hadley.

They smiled. Mary Rose, Hadley and Robbie said, "Cheese."

Marge, Wiley and Alphonso said, "Whiskey."

It was a good picture.

"Watch the one hundred twenty miles around Kluane Lake," a man said. He was wearing a University of Alabama sweatshirt. "It will jar everything loose in your RV."

Hadley made a mental note to double wrap the crystal.

They had lunch in an historic old café, looked through the Milepost Magazine Robbie had purchased at The Bookworm bookstore in Omaha, and had some of the best and strongest coffee of the trip so far.

You need some serious preparation to drive that road.

Robbie smiled at them, reached into her computer case and pulled out a beautiful, hard back book of Robert Service poems.

"I wanted the gold and I got it," Alphonso said as Robbie put the big book on their table and opened it. What she read was magic. There was *The Spell of the Yukon* and as she read the last stanza, they were all watching her with rapt attention. Without Robbie realizing it, the entire restaurant had become quiet, listening and watching.

It's the great, big, broad land 'way up yonder,
It's the forests where silence has lease;
It's the beauty that fills me with wonder,
It's the stillness that fills me with peace.

Still not aware that she was reading to a fairly good-sized crowd, Robbie read the entire *The Heart of the Sourdough* and went right on to the next page for *The Law of the Yukon.* When she looked up and took a breath she saw everyone looking at her in appreciation.

"Read *The Cremation of Sam McGee,*" a man with a Santa Claus beard said. Robbie was stunned. Everyone in the restaurant was nodding in encouragement. She smiled, turned a few pages and as she began the famous Service poem, three or four people began to recite it with her.

There are strange things done in the midnight sun
By the men who toil for gold;
The Arctic trails have their secret tales
That would make your blood run cold.

Three of the four people quoting with Robbie knew the first stanza right down to the last line and they said it loudly, "I cremated Sam McGee." Robbie grinned a shy grin and closed the book. The crowd applauded and a voice with a British accent said, "Right on there!"

"I love Robert Service," Robbie said, as she climbed into the driver's seat of the Hummer. The big car had become dusty by the time they crossed into Canada, and it seemed to be saying, "You ain't seen nothin' yet!" As Geoffrey wagged his tail at the egg Wiley slid into his bowl in the back compartment, his big tail hit the inside of the nearest window. Little clouds of dust and two tiny stones flew off into the air.

"Will you read us a Service poem every time we have dinner?" Mary Rose asked.

Robbie nodded. "Think of what it must have been like in the Malamute Saloon near Fairbanks, Alaska, when Robert Service sat there, writing about the Sourdoughs and the gold and the tough people who were there.

Marge pulled out her phone and asked for the phone number for the Malamute Saloon. The phone rang. A young voice on a recording machine told them the famous saloon was closed permanently.

“Crap,” Robbie, Hadley and Mary Rose said together.

There is a romance about the Yukon that captures you. Maybe it’s the spirit that caught Robert Service. Maybe it’s the midnight sun. Maybe it’s the color and intensity of the Northern Lights. Maybe it’s the ruggedness of the land. Maybe it’s the loneliness that covers it. Maybe it’s being called a Sourdough after you’ve survived for a year and made it through the dark winter. Whatever it was, the Yukon captured the six friends just as it had the great poet. They huddled closer together when they got out of their vehicles to stand at a viewing point. They talked softer at dinner. They loved it.

And each late afternoon, as they waited for their food to cook or waited in a restaurant to be served, Dr. Robinson Leary pulled out the hardback book and read another Robert Service poem.

If you’re looking for a sign, here it is.

“Who thought of this?” Wiley asked.

They were standing at the center of The Signpost Forest in Watson Lake, Yukon. They had come a total of 635 miles on the Alcan highway, stayed overnight at the Watson Lake Campground, and were walking through poles and fences covered with license plates and signs from towns all over the world. Some travelers made the trip just to put their town's sign on a post. It wound through a park and seemed to go on forever. They found two Nebraska license plates and one from Iowa.

"Makes Carhenge look wimpy," Alphonso said, thinking of the weird and mysterious group of cars standing on end in Nebraska.

"Come on," Marge said, "we're two days out of Gospel Bird. Let's move it."

Actually, though they didn't know it, they were three days out. A mild disaster was sneaking up on them - or was it TWO mild disasters?

Haines, Haines, the Gang's All Here

Alphonso was driving, his black van leading the little procession tooling down the highway. Robbie was reading from Milepost Magazine, and they drove straight through Haines Junction.

"Neat little place," Hadley observed.

"If we hadn't just had such a big breakfast in Whitehorse, we could stop for coffee," Marge said.

"I'm going to start asking about an Inukshuk," Mary Rose said.

"Listen to this," Robbie said. "Milepost says we need to be aware of our roads. The junction here can be tricky."

In just minutes their road curved gently and another, narrower road, went straight ahead. Alphonso turned the van into the curve and kept going.

"He must know where he's going," Marge said.

"The Canadians do NOT waste money on road signs," Hadley said.

She was right. None of them saw a highway number sign or a direction sign telling them what was down the road.

"It's okay," Robbie said. "We should be at Nugget City soon."

They drove on. Neither Nugget City or any other village appeared. Finally, they came to a wide spot in the road with a gas station and a Quonset hut. Three or four small houses were gathered around as though trying to figure how to get out of town.

"Must be it," Robbie said. "Nugget City? Not where the magazine says it is." She continued to look at the map, but nothing seemed to make sense.

"There's only one road," Marge said, "this has to be right."

They drove on. They hadn't caught sight of the rear end of the van for a long time.

There were no towns, but the scenery was, as usual spectacular.

"If you want to see the best view in the world," Hadley said, "just turn your head to your right."

Mary Rose smiled, “If you want the best view, turn your head to the left.”

While Alphonso had agreed that the journey was part of the fun, he drove as if he only wanted to get as far as he could in any given day. An hour passed, then two. Marge tried to call him, but there was no cell service. Geoffrey began to whine.

Mary Rose was driving. She pulled the Hummer and trailer into a small roadside stop with two porta-potties in it and they all got out.

“They’ll miss us eventually,” she predicted.

Geoffrey found a tree and the girls found the porta-potties.

Marge climbed into the trailer and brought out five energy bars.

They hit the road again.

In twenty miles they saw the van, parked in another pull out. The girls drove by, honked and waved and the van pulled onto the road behind them.

It was afternoon when they crossed into Alaska.

The young man at the border looked at their passports and wished them well.

"Where's the nearest campground?" Alphonso asked.

"In Haines," the border guard said, pointing down the road, "twelve miles,"

"Then we can find the road to Anchorage," Wiley said.

It was mid-afternoon when they arrived in the nice-sized town of Haines.

"Where the heck's the road?" Alphonso said as they parked on a side street and gathered around his van.

"Let's ask at the Visitor Center," Hadley said, pointing to an attractive building at the end of the street. They began to walk toward it. Alphonso went into the van and lowered his scooter.

Alphonso got his, "Where's the road?" question answered at the visitor center by an attractive young woman who looked at them with a definite, "idiots!" look in her eye. She smiled sweetly, however, and said, "The road is the road back. The one you came in on. You can take the ferry, but if you have two vehicles and a trailer there may be a space problem. You'll just have to go back to Haines Junction and go from there."

Tourists!

As her friends started toward the door, Mary Rose moved closer to the young woman. She smiled her best grandmotherly smile.

"My dear. Is there any place in Haines where I can get an Inukshuk?"

The young woman's face went blank.

"I have no idea what you're talking about."

Mary Rose smiled again. "Where are you from, dear?"

"Missouri,"

"I thought so," and she hurried out the door to catch up with the others.

They decided to explore Haines and since they had come 150 miles out of the way, stay overnight at a very nice campground.

Shops in Haines were delightful and quaint. At each one Mary Rose cornered a clerk and asked about Inukshuks. In each one, no one had a clue what she meant. She did, however, meet people from, Iowa, Kansas, California, Alberta, Winnipeg and most often - Texas.

“Okay,” Hadley said after Mary Rose’s fifth unsuccessful attempt in her Inukshuk hunt, “I’ve held out as long as I can. Robbie, Mary Rose, what is an Inukshuk?”

Robbie smiled, “They’re fabulous,” she said, “native Alaskan people made human-like figures out of rocks to mark where there was game or where the native peoples of the Arctic should be aware of something. They are big flat and round rocks put together to make a human-like form. Some are huge, always big in the snows of the Arctic.” She pulled out her smart phone and found a YouTube video of an Inuit Inukshuk builder.

Hadley watched, rapt. “I want one!” she said.

“Me, too,” Robbie nodded.

“Mary Rose,” Hadley said when they climbed into the Hummer, “how do you know about Inukshuks?”

"I had a friend who took the Alaskan cruise and brought one home. My husband went on a business trip to Skagway years and years ago," Mary Rose said. "He brought me one. You've seen it. It sits on that shelf under my television."

Robbie and Hadley looked at each other, did a small eye roll together and shrugged.

Amazing what you don't notice.

As they ate dinner in The Hungry Moose Bar and Grill in Haines, Mary Rose had a suggestion. "Tonight is Saturday and it's only three hours..."

Only THREE HOURS! the others thought.

"Only three hours back to Haines. Let's all go to a nice Catholic church tomorrow."

"Is there an Episcopal?" Hadley asked.

"Baptist?" Alphonso said.

"United Methodist?" Robbie suggested.

"Presbyterian?" Marge put in.

They looked at Wiley expectantly, "Orthodox Heathen," He replied.

"Okay," Robbie said, "Let's drive around about ten o'clock in the morning and the first church we come to is the one we attend."

They agreed.

Theology of the Snow Machine

That night it snowed.

It was one of Alaska's heavy, slow, wet, spring storms; not a lot, but enough to measurably add to the hard pack snow that was already on the ground and to blow some of the wet stuff into drifts against the buildings of the campground.

They walked carefully to the Hummer and were glad they had unhooked the tow bar the day before. Robbie shook one foot when snow slipped inside her shoe.

Geoffrey watched longingly from a window in the trailer. He had tried to play in the snow when Wiley took him out earlier, but Wiley was in a hurry.

Humans are always in a hurry.

They have no appreciation of playing in the snow or sniffing trees.

It didn't take them long to find a church. Alphonso turned a corner in the Hummer, went up a little back road and there, next to n a Dead-End sign, almost hidden among some beautiful big pine trees, was a charming log cabin church with a big sign out front.

He parked in the one handicapped parking space, hooked his handicapped sign on the rear-view mirror and they got out.

As he balanced on his two canes he noticed that there were more snowmobiles parked along the street in front of the church than there were cars. In fact, there were NO cars. The only vehicles were snowmobiles and pickup trucks. Alphonso shook his head.

Alaska all right.

Their timing must have been good because a few people were making their way up the neatly shoveled and salted walk to the big, rustic front doors of the church. As they turned onto the sidewalk leading to those doors, they stopped to read the sign and find out what church they had won by the luck of the 'first one we find' draw. It was a big sign, too big for the size of the little church. What it said was in big letters, as well.

Fundamental Pentecostal Holiness
Church of the True Baptism

And beneath that, in big black letters on a white background were the words:

One way
The Only Way
And it's OUR way.

"I doubt they do blessings of the animals," Robbie observed.

"Bet they do blessing of the snow mobiles," Alphonso said, coming up behind them.

"Oh, this is going to be interesting," their Orthodox Heathen grinned, and he pointed to the name of the pastor, written in gold letters, no less, at the bottom of the sign.

The Right Reverent D. Festus Middlefinger,
True Apostle.

They went inside.

The church was simple. The pews were traditional uncomfortable wood, three different hymnals rested in racks on the back of each pew along with a ream-sized book of typing paper with "The Gospel of D. Festus Middlefinger" again, in big letters, on the first page that acted as a cover. At the front of the church, framing the pulpit that planted itself in the middle of the altar area were three flags: The United States, with a bronze eagle on top of the flagpole, the Christian flag, with an old rugged cross on top and the Alaskan flag with a tiny silver bear perched like a bird at the end of the flagpole. "I like the bear best," Mary Rose whispered to Wiley.

The impressive thing about the altar and pulpit, however, was a large, deadly -looking sword fastened threateningly onto the front of the pulpit.

"What's he going to do with that sword?" Hadley whispered to Marge.

"I don't know, but I'm keeping my cane on Taser just in case."

The two men had noticed the sword as well.

"I hope they don't do circumcisions," Wiley whispered.

Alphonso smothered a laugh.

Theology built on necessity.

They read the large, unwieldy bulletin.

"Oh, my Gosh!" Robbie whispered, "look at these hymns, they're all printed out, but they aren't really hymns." She leaned over to show them to Hadley. "This is NOT Blessed Assurance."

"Blessed Insurance," Hadley read softly. "I pay with a smile.

My snow machine's covered, my bathroom is tile."

It continued like that for four painful stanzas.

The congregation stood when a piano in the back began to play. Mary Rose turned to sneak a peek and saw a skinny, nimble woman, Mrs. Middlefinger perhaps, attack the keyboard with a sweep of the keys. They sang Blessed Insurance ad they sang it loudly.

D. Festus Middlefinger walked to the pulpit. He was a little less than six feet tall, bald with a rim of white hair and a thin, very long, white beard that ended in a point over his chest.

Wiley leaned over to Alphonso, "If he has a box of snakes behind that pulpit, grab that sword."

"I'm grabbing Marge's cane!" Alphonso whispered back.

They were seated in the middle of the church, but no one sat near them or greeted them. The pew behind them was empty. The pew in front of them was empty. Everyone in the church was dressed in snow suits and boots.

The Reverend Middlefinger looked over his

congregation, smiled a rather greasy smile, nodded to the six obvious visitors and opened a large Bible that rested on the pulpit - his Bible with Middlefinger gospels. He began to speak in a calm, somewhat ordinary voice.

In the gospel of Festus, chapter 2 verses the Dallas Cowboys, it is written 'Blessed are the blessed.' Blessed are those who are blest real good… and you and I know what that means because we live here, here in this sacred land of Blessedness. Look around . . . the mountains, the sky, the roads filled with old geezers in RVs going 30 miles an hour . . .and most of all (he held the truth as one about to sneeze) our snowmobiles. God gave us snowmobiles. It is the full expression of our divine right as Alaskans to the spoils of the earth. And what is the root of "spoil" but "oil" and what is the outcome of oil in Alaska, but our annual blessed dividends and the snow machines they buy.

Mary Rose leaned toward Robbie, "Dividends?"

Robbie nodded. "Every member of each Alaska household gets $1,100 annually, sometimes more, sometimes less, from oil revenues."

Mary Rose nodded. "Cool!"

A woman two pews in front of them turned and frowned.

O sure, there are some who dividend in Hawaii and some who dividend with a new behemoth truck, but the true manifestation of the Hebrew word "Yamaha" is "Go like hell through snow." Snow machines, YES! IditaGod and bought a snow job.

Some people look at me and shout, "That's him! He's a snow Job." And I reply with my family name . . .No. . . NO, I am not a snow job, but I ride one. I am not a big fish in small stream, but I catch them. I cannot see Russia from my back porch, but I can rush-a from my house like a bat out of hell...with this year's new "God model" Skidoo.

Rev. Middlefinger, caught his breath and then took another good look at the morning's congregation.

Now, this morning we have visitors here in Haines. I can tell. I can tell they are visitors by their blank stares. They look like folk from New Jersey, staring at a plate full of grits. They look more than B-fuddled, or even C. or D. fuddled. They look like folks who have gasped their last fud. Do you know what “fud” means in the ancient Greek.? It means “What da hell?”

Marge leaned toward Alphonso, “I don’t think he’s talking about Hell,” she whispered. “I think this preacher swears!”

To these visitors this morning that is the question. But to us in Alaska we know the answer: snow machines. That is who we are. That is what God called us to embrace, that is our mission in the church of the True Baptism.

Last year we sent two snow machines to Puerto Rico . . . why? Because Jesus on a snow machine, WE CARE! When folks come to visit us driving 80-foot RVs we care . . .We care you are here . . . because RVs drink gas like a hole in the tank and gas means oil and more oil means more dividends and more dividends means more snow machines!

The congregation applauded. Wiley, who had dozed off, jumped awake.

Why did Lottie B. Moan give birth last week in her garage? She wanted the blessing of baby with the snow machine. Why was Harry Dotard cremated with his Yamaha? Must

I say? Then again, let's make note: When cremated with your snow mobile, remember to drain the gas tank. Someone on cruise ship was hit by a flying foot.

Mary Rose gasped and put her hand over her heart.

We are a snow machine people. Like it said in the book of Norge, "What does it profit a man to have a good snow if he cannot go?

Reverend Middlefinger gave a sweeping motion with his arm and they stood again for the last hymn.

"Oh, Sweet Jesus!" Robbie groaned. "My favorite and they've desecrated it."

"In the Bleak Midwinter
Snow on snow on snow
Bless our snow mobiles, God
Bless us as we go."

As the music filled the little church, the six friends hurried up the aisle and out the door to avoid Reverend Middlefinger who, in minutes, would be at that door shaking hands. They rushed to the Hummer as fast as safety allowed, climbed in and Alphonso backed out and burned rubber down the wet street where melting snow was running into the sewers.

As they turned onto a second street to head back to the campground, Mary Rose said, "Look! The street sign says the church is on True Redemption Alley."

They hitched up the trailer, Geoffrey bounded around in the snow that was starting to seriously melt now, and they shot up the road toward Haines Junction and the real Alcan highway, which was one hundred and fifty miles away.

On the Road, On the Road
Who Knows when we'll Arrive?

They hit the bad stretch of road predicted by the University of Alabama gentleman when they were in Dawson Creek. It happened just as they passed Destruction Bay.

"Fitting name!" Robbie said loudly as she bounced in her seat. She couldn't tell if her travel mates were nodding in agreement or bouncing themselves.

Winter had done a number on the highway. Huge, oversized road equipment rumbled or sat at the ready alongside the big road. Men and women in orange vests were everywhere. Traffic was creeping and bumping along.

Hadley had double wrapped the crystal.

After one really bad hole in the road, someone had erected a big sign that read, "You'll never get there on time. Ha, Ha, Ha."

In ten more rough, mean miles, another sign read, "There is a highway to Hell and only a stairway to Heaven. Welcome to the highway."

Geoffrey didn't like this ride. He dug his claws into what was usually a warm, comforting, oversized doggie bed and whined when his food and water bowl slid by him in his compartment. He looked at his ladies. They were all hanging onto their seats.

No, he did not like this ride at all!

A woman in one of the orange vests flagged them down. They were near the edge of an unbelievably steep detour that had been carved into a narrow space at the side of the road. If you went off it, you were falling down a massive drop on the passenger side. It was made up of an extremely steep, narrow hill, with a very short, straight and narrow piece of temporary highway that looked as if it wasn't even big enough for a semi-trailer, then an equally steep, impossible grade that put you back onto the main highway where the huge machines were rattling and steaming with work and threatening to roll over any vehicle that didn't make it through the detour and got in the way.

Wiley and Alphonso were in the van right behind the Hummer. They could see this vicious-looking man-made detour. They could see Geoffrey when he stood up as soon as they stopped for the flag, looked out the back window at them and barked pitifully. They watched as he turned in a circle and threw up.

"Bummer," Wiley said.

"He's scared, too," Alphonso answered.

"You think I should go offer to drive the Hummer down that thing?"

Alphonso looked at him in amazement from his position behind the wheel.

"You want to get out of this van, go up to Marge Aaron, retired homicide detective, Marge Aaron, who can Taser, shoot, knife and smoke screen you out of existence and you are going to ask her if she needs help driving?"

Wiley shrugged. "Dumb idea, right?"

Alphonso grinned. "You have a death wish, buddy? You want to die?"

A monster 18-wheeler made a huge bang as something underneath it hit when it began its climb up the short, steep detour hill.

"Like a mini Lombard Street," Hadley said.

They were totally quiet as the flag woman motioned Marge to begin the decent.

They braced their feet and held on. Geoffrey followed suit and braced all four feet.

The tow-bar between the Hummer and trailer banged.

Something else made a loud metal-on-metal noise.

Mary Rose realized she was holding her breath.

“Oh Crap!” Marge said as a tire hit a large rock and they skidded a little toward the deep ravine on the passenger side.

“Yikes!” Hadley said.

Geoffrey yelped.

“Holy Moly!” Robbie yelled.

“Hail Mary, full of grace...” Mary Rose began, then became silent again.

Marge stepped on the gas, gunned the motor and went up the steep hill with more banging and clanking and breath holding.

Hadley had images of broken crystal that, like visions of sugarplums, danced in her head.

They made it to the top and watched as Alphonso maneuvered the van, also banging and clanking, up the detour.

"That woman with the flag laughed at us," Mary Rose announced.

They looked at her.

"Stop at the next pull out," Hadley said. "I have to pee."

Mary Rose shook her head, "YOU have to pee! Why do you think my legs are crossed?"

Three days later, when they pulled into the Chicken Little Campground in Gospel Bird, Alaska, they were exhausted. The van, Hummer and trailer were covered and caked with dirt and grime. A piece was missing from the Hummer's grill and there was a dent in the side of the van and another in the side of the trailer.

They had driven the Alcan highway.

Geoffrey was so tired of riding that he had tried to run away, but when Mary Rose started to cry, he ran back, licked her face and jumped into his compartment.

Hadley could hardly see; the sun had been so bright that even her especially made dark lenses hadn't helped.

Robbie and Marge had argued about something. They never argued, and now they couldn't remember what had made them disagree.

Hadley's hands had been shaking when she checked the crystal. Nothing was broken and none of the other girls could understand why she started to cry. If they had been back at Meadow Lakes, everyone would have been sympathetic and known what the tears were all about.

Wiley and Alphonso had avoided arguments and tears by making sure whoever wasn't driving was either asleep or pretending to be.

Mary Rose had asked everywhere they stopped if anyone knew where she could get an Inuksuk. No one knew what she was talking about, but she met more people who were employed in Alaska. These were from Rhode Island, San Diego, Des Moines, Iowa, Minnesota, South Dakota, Utah and Virginia.

The Coziest Cell in Alaska

They all felt better the next day. Alphonso was calling around to find a body shop that worked on RVs and vans and was finding a surprising number of them. "And surprise, surprise, they all sell tires," he announced.

By lunch time they had begun to feel human again and were ready to go into Gospel Bird to meet Buckshot Betsy Bushwhacker. Except for Alphonso, they were all in jeans and boots and almost, but not quite, looked as if they belonged in Alaska.

"There's the jail," Robbie pointed out as they drove down main street. Just two blocks further on was a restaurant called The Ill Eagle. They parked and went in.

The restaurant was rustic with mounted elk heads, deer heads and one large rabbit with fake antlers on the walls. The tables were mixed and matched with the chairs and there was a large wood-burning stove at one end. It was dark, even though the front sported large, attractive windows. They ordered from the breakfast menu and were served by a waitress who had a name tag that simply read, "Waitress."

"What's your name, dear?" Hadley asked,

smiling at the young woman..

“Waitress,” the girl replied, a big smile on her well-lipsticked lips.

“No,” Hadley smiled wider, “I mean your real name.”

The waitress grinned wider as well, “That IS my real name. My great-grandma was in a café in Anchorage years and years ago and she saw this woman with ‘Waitress’ on her name tag and Great Granny thought that was the most beautiful name, so I’m the third generation of Waitresses in my family.”

They looked at her and now they all smiled.

Robbie put her head down and did an eye roll toward the salt and pepper shakers.

“We knew a charming young server who had a name tag that read, ‘Hey Miss,’” Hadley told her. “That’s what everyone called her when she was serving.”

“I like that, too,” Waitress said.

Mary Rose broke in. “Waitress where can I get an Inuksuk?”

"If you go down the Cassair Highway on your way home, there's a place called Jade City and they have lots. Otherwise, museums and gift shops? They used to be all over the place, but I haven't seen any for years." She put her hand on Mary Rose's shoulder. "'Course if you want to see real ones, you have to go to the Arctic." She laughed and left to give their orders to the cook.

"Ah Ha!" Mary Rose said. "A native!"

"With a great name," Marge said. Her cane was comfortably hanging on the back of her chair. Everyone was comfortable in the warm, cozy restaurant. Geoffrey was comfortable waiting in the Hummer, his head on his food bowl, his nose sniffing the good meat smells from the place where his people had gone. It was all down-right comforting.

He was a good dog.

He should have been allowed to go into the Ill Eagle, too.

Humans!

The meal was delicious and they all agreed that this would be their regular eating place in Gospel Bird.

They left the restaurant and stopped at the Hummer. Mary Rose gave the egg she had saved and half a piece of toast to Geoffrey and they decided to walk down the street one block to the jail. They walked slowly so Alphonso's canes could keep up.

The jail looked like a refugee from an old "Bonanza" TV episode. When they went inside, Manley Malaprop was a similar, but stupid-looking version of Bonanza's Hoss Cartwright and Hoss Cartwright had never looked brilliant.

"Did you know Hoss' name was really Eric Cartwright?" Wiley said to Alphonso.

"I did not know that," Alphonso smiled. "Like Hoss better."

The jail smelled musty and moldy with just a light tone of lavender mixed in. It was fair sized, but junky and generally unkept. Manley stood up behind his desk and showed his full height, which was considerable. Alphonso caned his way over to him to show him he was bigger, by a long shot, held out his hand, introduced himself and crushed Manley's hand in his big paw.

"Down Hoss, down," Hadley whispered to Robbie. "Our guy's got you."

A line of sweat broke out on Manley's forehead and Alphonso smiled his biggest smile.

"Sheriff, it's good to meet you and have your cooperation and assistance. Let me introduce you." Alphonso named off his friends, Marge held her cane forward on her arm, even though it was just a cane with jewels on it to Manley, and finally the sheriff pointed to a row of three cells behind them,

They turned and looked at the cell block of the Gospel Bird jail.

"In there," he said, giving Alphonso a look of pure envy.

As soon as they turned they saw, standing in the unlocked door of her cell, Buckshot Betsy Bushwhacker. They had been so intent on annoying Sheriff Malaprop that they hadn't paid any attention to the actual cells.

Manley's grandmother and her ladies had transformed the cell into a dorm room with class. There was a gingham privacy curtain in reds and blues with white trim that could be pulled around three sides of the cell to provide privacy in the tiny space. They had installed a toilet seat and made a matching cover for the lid. Betsy's cot had a thick mattress that actually looked soft and plush and covering the mattress was a beautiful, hand-sewn crazy quilt. A braided rug softened the concrete floor. The bridge ladies had made a matching pillow cover and embroidered their names on it.

It could have come from a magazine named, "Cell Beautiful."

When they said the cell looked pretty, Betsy told them the ladies had tried to decorate the jailhouse shower, but the two drunks who stayed overnight on weekends had complained about the body wash and plastic curtain with mermaids on it.

When Manley had been brave enough to confront all four women at once and tell them they had to take everything down from the shower, they glared at him and the mermaid curtain had stayed.

Never underestimate four burned out old broads.

In a corner of the little cell was a large basket filled with books and magazines. A small candle under the sink gave out the delicious lavender scent. An ornate antique mirror hung over the sink and one of Betsy's pictures she had drawn hung over the toilet. Immediately outside the door, leaning gracefully up against Betsy's cell, was a brand-new card table and four matching chairs.

"I wanna thank you all for comin;" Betsy almost yelled.

Marge moved forward and gave her a big hug.

It was easy to see they were related. Betsy was as tall as Marge with the same brown, curly hair Marge had five years ago when they first met her at Meadow Lakes. Now, Marge's curls were mostly gray. The big difference was that Betsy's hair was long and spun into a French braid that hung to her waist. While Marge was a big woman who should be big, Betsy was big-boned and thin. She wore no makeup and her dress was plain and long, almost to the floor. On the front of her dress was an old-fashioned peace symbol worn by hippies more than forty years ago. The dress looked as vintage as Betsy herself, and her ankle-high boots were lined with fur and well worn.

Wiley brought the four chairs into the cell. It was crowded but cozy. They could see their reflections in the big mirror. Mary Rose straightened her hair as she looked in it.

Alphonso, Hadley, Robbie and Mary Rose sat in the chairs. Marge sat on the cot with her cousin and Wiley took his place on the gingham toilet seat.

Some men have a natural taste for sweet and cute.

Betsy went over her sad story again. She hadn't meant to kill PickAxe, he was going to shoot the lock off on her door, he had threatened her and tried to beat her a few times. Each time she had basically beat the crap out of him instead. She was going to scare him away. She fired high. What it all came down to was that it was his fault because he wore stupid-looking boots with high heels and lifts.

"Like KISS," Alphonso, Marge, Hadley and Robbie said together.

Buckshot looked at them and blinked away her confusion.

"So, like I say," she repeated, "it's his own varmity fault for bein' so vain and weariin' those stupid boots!"

Marge put her hand on Buckshot's knee. "As a retired homicide detective, I've never heard that work as a defense. It isn't the victim's fault you shot him."

"But I didn't AIM at him!" Betsy insisted.

"Varmity?" Mary Rose leaned over and whispered to Wiley.

"As in being a varmint," he whispered back.

Mary Rose nodded and did an eye roll. Alphonso changed the subject. "Tell us about the prosecutor."

"Slik Quick," Buckshot sneered. "Another varmint. Got deserted by Ditcher and Hyde of Ditcher Quick and Hyde, Attorneys at Law. Got to be prosecutor because he's the only lawyer in town. Dumb as a rock." She snorted, and this time Betsy did an eye roll.

That looked familiar.

"And what about your defense attorney?" Alphonso asked.

"Don't have one," Betsy replied, looking down at the braided rug the ladies had put on her floor.

"Oh great," Marge said. "If Slik is the only act in town, where do we get a defense attorney who doesn't live on a dirt road a hundred miles away?"

"Manley's grandma looked into it for me." Betsy said. "She finally called Judge Judge to see who he knew, and he just told her, 'Good luck. Let me know if you find one.' Most of his criminals defend themselves and end up in jail so he'd like to know a couple of good shysters himself."

They were all quiet.

Things didn't look good.

Then Alphonso spoke up," How about Raven?" he asked, glancing sheepishly at Robbie.

They looked at him, then they looked at Robbie.

"Raven's a lawyer?" Robbie almost yelled. "He never told me!"

"Probably didn't ask him," Alphonso said. "Apaches don't talk much. Graduated from Boston University School of Law. Worked out west for a few years with a firm he started called Raven, Robyn and Byrd."

"You've got to be kidding!" Robbie wailed.

"Nope," was all Alphonso said.

Robbie pulled out her smart phone and told it to, "Call Raven."

The way she said it wasn't friendly.

The smart phone did what it was told to do.

Raven, the Apache, answered on the first ring. He didn't say anything which is his normal greeting.

"Are you a lawyer?" Robbie yelled into the phone.

"I am," they heard him answer.

Robbie ran her hand through her hair and brought her voice under control.

"Well then, talk to your football buddy," and she shoved the phone toward Alphonso.

"Hey, Man, you want a fun case?" Alphonso asked. Then he laughed.

As they left the jail, Manley Malaprop stopped them.

"You have to call me first before you visit my prisoner," He sneered. "This jail has its rules."

"Taser him, Marge," Mary Rose whispered. "Go ahead, Taser him."

"Can't do that," Marge said.

She looked at Wiley, holding the door open while Alphonso and the girls walked out.

As Manley turned and started walking to his desk, Marge pressed one of the jewels on her cane. Tripping pellets shot out onto the floor, most of them rolling in front of the sheriff. Marge gave Mary Rose, who was just starting out the door, a gentle push and hurried out herself as fast as her knee would allow, quickly closing the door behind them.

They heard a loud thunk and an even louder, "Ow!" from Manley as his big body hit the floor.

"I hate when I accidentally hit one of those buttons," Marge sighed.

Robbie, Hadley and Mary Rise did eye rolls and giggled, Wiley and Alphonso did a high five, and they headed down the street toward the Hummer.

Part Four

Beautiful Jewels: Human and Gem

From: *The BOOB Girls: The Musical-* Mary Rose is getting her makeover and new hair style and she and the girls are deciding they are beautiful.

(Peyton Claireborne, Master Hair Stylist sings to Mary Rose McGill)

I can see there's a lot to be undone
And I don't mean just the hair.
We have got to remove the restraints which have kept your life empty and bare.

Maybe you were taught to silence the song your heart was meant to sing.
Maybe your special rose never bloomed from a cold and cloudy spring.

But no matter, that's all in the past, time to choose something new.
No more hiding the radiance of your heart, time to let out the genuine you.

Because you're Beautiful!
Beautiful and meant to be free.
Because what I tell you is true,

You're beautiful, beautiful, beautiful!
You're meant to be You!

(The Girls)
So our faces are chiseled by time
and sculpted by years.
We have earned every wrinkle and line
with our love and our laughter and tears.
Maybe we've been told loveliness,
blossoms only in youth.
Our years- each one has seen the flowering of a
much greater truth.

Let's acknowledge the wonder we've become.
Let us affirm every part.
No more hiding our consummate charm
because
We're beautiful!
We are time's work of art.
We're beautiful, beautiful, beautiful.
It's all there to see.
We're beautiful and meant to be free.
We're beautiful, beautiful, beautiful
And meant to be free!

More Precious than Rubies

Alphonso found a body shop that could take the van, the Hummer and the trailer in the same day. They would finish the van first, so the men could spend the night in it. The trailer and Hummer would take two days.

They ate breakfast at the Ill Eagle, with Waitress as their waitress.

“Where can we stay overnight in Gospel Bird while our vehicles get fixed?” Hadley asked her.

Waitress smiled, “Well there’s the well-decorated jail, and you’d be close to Buckshot there.”

Hadley smiled back, and Waitress went on. “There’s the Sunrise Motel and it’s fine if you don’t mind a bedbug or two. The Sunset Motel is on the other side of town, and it rents rooms by the hour. Probably the only okay place to stay would be in Wander Lost.”

“You mean Wanderlust?” Robbie suggested.

“No,” Waitress said, “it’s Wander Lost. An old bed and breakfast on the north road out of town.”

There was only one road out of town and it ran north. Didn't have a name. Didn't need one.

"Do we need reservations?" Hadley asked.

Waitress laughed.........and laughed.

"Let's go," Alphonso said.

It took less than an hour for the girls to pack enough clothes, makeup and medicines for one night and perhaps two, if the body shop didn't come through in two days as promised.

"It will be nice to be out of the trailer for a couple of days," Mary Rose said.

Geoffrey was standing near her and taking up most of the bedroom area she shared with Robbie, watching and hoping. Suitcases sometimes meant fun.

"It will indeed be good to be trailer-free," Robbie agreed.

"I know I'm getting old when it takes me longer to pack my medicine than my makeup," Hadley observed.

"And it's exciting to pack knee braces," Marge grumbled.

"Growing old sucks!" Mary Rose said.

They nodded, then Mary Rose smiled. "SHIT!" she grinned.

They laughed and straightened up over their suitcases. Their good posture was short-lived. They all bent over at the same time and kept packing.

Wiley had driven the Hummer behind Alphonso and they dropped off the van. As the girls finished packing, they heard Wiley hitching up the Hummer to the trailer.

"Hang on!" Marge yelled as he backed into the tow cap. "They must not know we're in here."

Mary Rose opened the door and yelled at Wiley, "Watch it, Cute Stuff!"

He laughed.

"I'm going to try to get Geoff into the Bed and Breakfast," Mary Rose said. Geoffrey was in his compartment in the Hummer, his head over the seat, resting comfortably on Mary Rose's shoulder. "If the boys kept him, they'd lead him astray and he'd never be the same."

They grinned.

Robbie reached over the seat and patted the big mastiff.

They drove for about five miles on the road known as the road north.

When they came to a little pull out with a picnic table and porta-potty, Mary Rose spoke up, "Alphonso, pull over, will you? I want to let Geoffrey find a tree."

Alphonso pulled over. They all got out to look at a beautiful view seen from the pull out's scenic overlook at the top of the hill.

Geoffrey sniffed three trees before he found the right one.

Then he sniffed around the roots.

"Come on, Geoffrey," Mary Rose said, and she pulled on his leash.

He held firm, his nose glued to the ground.

"Geoffrey!" Mary Rose said.

As Wiley started to move toward the big dog to take his collar, Geoffrey began to dig.

There is something about a big, short-haired monster dog that makes digging a living art.

His front feet pumped. Dirt flew in every direction.

Mary Rose jumped backward and would have fallen if Wiley hadn't been beside her to grab her arm.

Chunks of dirt hit Wiley's shirt.

Alphonso, who had waited in the driver's seat of the Hummer, grabbed his canes and hurried to the group, all of whom had stepped back a step, even the girls who weren't close to Geoffrey's new project.

Marge made her way toward Geoffrey, speaking softly, "Geoffrey, hey good dog, what's going on, big guy? Let us see. You got a clue there?"

You can take the girl out of the homicide division, but you can't take the homicide division out of the girl.

Geoffrey put his muzzle into the sizeable hole he had created and came up with a delicate chain in his teeth. His mouth was covered with mud, his ears were covered with mud and even his big eyebrows were mud-encrusted.

He looked at them as if he had won an Olympic gold medal.

Marge reached out and took the chain from his mouth. She looked at it and at what was on it. "It's like one of those old heart lockets that carry little photographs inside, but this one isn't a heart like those are."

She walked carefully over the rough ground to the group that had gathered on the other side of the hole. Her knee hurt, and she swore at it under her breath.

Geoffrey busied himself cleaning off his face with his bear-sized paws.

They gathered around and looked at the locket. It was, indeed, not a heart but a beautiful little treasure chest, of good size for a locket. The top of the chest was made up of tiny red jewels. The lower part of the chest was decorated in equally tiny blue gems. Three were missing and looked as if they had been gone for years.

"I'd call it a necklace, not just a locket," Hadley said. "It's too big." She held out her hand and Marge put the necklace in it.

"Wow!" Hadley said. She looked at her friends. "If I'm right, these little jewels here? They're rubies and sapphires. This is worth some money."

She tried to pry it open, but it had obviously been buried and locked for years. Finally, Wiley took out his pocket knife, put the blade into the lock. It gave a tiny click and opened.

"There's a paper in there!" Mary Rose said.

Robbie looked at Marge. "How does she do it?" she asked. "Nine years ago, she peed on a foot and found it was attached to a dead body. Now she sets her dog on a tree and finds..."

"A treasure map!" Mary Rose yelled.

They looked.

Sure enough, as Hadley gently lifted out the little paper, which was folded into a minuscule square, they could see it was marked with tiny drawings of landmarks and a small, red "X" in one corner.

All lines led to the little "X".

"Holy Moly," Robbie said.

"Well I'll be," Wiley and Alphonso said together.

"Sweet Jesus!" Marge whispered.

And Mary Rose McGill looked at the little map and uttered her usual, "Jesus, Mary and Joseph."

Sensing that he had done something good, Geoffrey barked once, shook vigorously to get more dirt off. and farted.

They moved into the sunlight and looked at the delicate, yellowed little map. At the bottom of the map was a drawing of a house with three pillars. A line leading to the right had a drawing of an old cabin and from there, a line went to a hill with what looked like a cave in the hill's steep side.

Hadley refolded the map carefully, so as not to tear the ancient paper, and handed it to Alphonso. "Here, Chief," she said. "Keep it safe."

"And make a copy," Marge said.

"Be careful not to lose it," Mary Rose added.

Robbie looked at Hadley and smiled, "Save that 'Chief' talk until the real Indian gets here."

Hadley laughed, put her arm around Robbie, and they all walked back to the Hummer.

Wander Lost

It was another long, winding, hilly five miles up the north road until they got to a battered sign that read:

Wander Lost
Bed and Breakfast
2 Miles
You are now found

"Everything from Canada through Alaska is always two miles away," Mary Rose said, shaking her head. "Rest area -2 miles, Scenic pull out - 2 miles, port a-potty - 2 miles."

They stopped at the side of the road when the somewhat accurate two miles was up. There, across the road on their left was a huge old mansion. Its three towering stories looked sturdy and solid. A widow's walk adorned the roof. Massive pines surrounded it.

"Good windbreak, those pines," Wiley said.

The windows were clean and boasted tasteful shutters. The entire house was painted a pale yellow. The lawn was immaculate and nicely landscaped. It was bordered by an iron fence with an ornate gate.

"It looks like Birdie's Nest cleaned up," Robbie sad.

Four years ago, Robinson Leary had received a letter from the city attorneys of Salem's Crossing, Nebraska. The attorneys, Butts, McCracken and Rears, informed her that she had inherited a bed and breakfast from a great aunt. There were only two problems: Robbie had never heard of this great aunt who would be over one hundred years old, and the big mansion that had been called, "Birdie's Nest" was in wrack and run. On top of that, for some time they were sure it was haunted.

Hadley, Mary Rose and Marge nodded in agreement. They remembered the old bed and breakfast and how rain would pound against the windows, but when they opened the door to check on the storm, all was dry outside.

Now they were at another ancient mansion and the only difference appeared to be orderliness.

"Uh oh," Marge said. "Alphonso, let's take a look at that map."

Alphonso dug the necklace and map out of his shirt pocket and handed them to Marge. She opened the necklace and unfolded the old map carefully.

"Look." She held the map up for them to see. "The house with three pillars," and she pointed to Wander Lost.

They looked, and Mary Rose gasped softly. Sure enough, the beautiful wrap-around porch on the old mansion had three ornately carved pillars decorating the front.

"It's on the treasure map," Hadley said.

"Let's go in and see if there's a ghost like at Salem's Crossing." Marge replied.

Alphonso turned into the circular drive in front of the mansion. He stopped the Hummer in front of the door, and he and Wiley started to get out with the girls.

"Huh un," Marge said, "this is girl stuff. We don't need you two. Go – take the van in and get a couple of copies made of that map."

They grabbed their overnight bags, Mary Rose grabbed Geoffrey and Marge slammed the back compartment door shut.

"Sure they'll take your puppy?" Wiley asked.

"They'll take him," Mary Rose said loudly. "We've overpowered houses like this before."

It was true. They had turned the old B&B in Salem's Crossing into a show place, rousted the "ghost," and arrested a kidnapper.

Never underestimate a burned out old broad.

Mary Rose led Geoffrey up the stairs close beside her. Marge grabbed ahold of the railing and pulled her aching knee up the stairs behind Hadley and Robbie.

It was Mary Rose who rang the bell.

A loud gong sounded.

They jumped. Geoffrey took a step backward.

The door opened immediately, as if someone had been standing on the other side, watching them and...waiting.

"You rang?"

They gasped. Standing before them was a gaunt man in what looked to be a black butler's uniform; or was it an undertaker's suit? He was almost seven feet tall. His hair was thin and wispy; one eye was blue, the other a pale grey. His hands looked like giant ham hocks.

Without thinking, together they said, "Lurch!"

He looked exactly like the Charles Addams character from the "Addams Family" television series - a cross between Frankenstein's monster and an oversized zombie.

The Lurch man growled softly, and Geoffrey growled back - more softly and from one careful step back.

Hadley made the next move. "We'd like rooms for tonight and possibly one more night," she said, and her voice was almost normal. Only the girls could detect a tiny squeak.

The others nodded, and Marge put her hand on the red cane resting over her arm. Geoffrey moved behind Mary Rose and whined.

"No dogs," the man said, glaring at Geoffrey. Or maybe that was his normal look and he just glared naturally. Geoffrey looked at Mary Rose.

"He's a service dog," Mary Rose said, taking a step forward.

The service dog moved even closer behind her, getting so close he was almost pushing her over.

"And what does he service, Mum?"

"He helps my anxiety," Mary Rose said quickly. "I have terrible anxiety attacks like the one I'm feeling coming on right now!" She crossed her eyes, stuck her tongue out a tiny bit and shook her head.

She looked to her friends for help.

"Terrible attacks," Hadley said.

"Truly sad," Robbie said.

"Have to call 911," Marge added.

Lurch looked at them as if they were bugs he'd like to squash. He still hadn't opened the door all the way.

Robbie thought about calling Alphonso and Wiley, then remembered there was no cell service.

They were trapped.

"My name is Login," the man said with a slight bow, and a larger glare at the service dog. "Welcome to Wander Lost."

“Thank you, Login,” Hadley said. She pronounced it Low-gin.

“No, Mum, it is pronounced Log in, as in what one does when one is signing into one’s stock portfolio on the internet. Log in.”

Robbie leaned toward Marge. “‘Thing’ is the password,”

“‘Cousin Itt’ is the user ID,” Marge whispered back.

There was no question that Login heard them.

“It is a fine Russian name,” Login frowned. “Many of us here are descendants of the Romanovs, rulers of Russia for generations.”

More like descendants of Rasputin, Robbie thought. She didn’t say anything, but she looked at Marge and Marge nodded.

Thinking the same thing.

“What is your last name, Login?” Hadley asked.

That’s it. Make friendly with the impossible.

The butler straightened up even taller. “I am

Login Knockemoff," he said with obvious pride. "Jesus, Mary and Joseph," Mary Rose whispered. And with that prayer to support them, they went through the door Login was holding open for them. Geoffrey worked his way around until he was exactly between Mary Rose and Marge. He was panting with anxiety.

The dog who helps with anxiety attacks.

The mansion was extremely tastefully decorated. A Persian rug of obvious worth covered the entryway. An antique table, with "expensive" written all over it, sat in the center of the rug and held a huge bouquet of cut flowers. The flowers had been expensive, too. Chairs were strategically placed around the room, and Hadley guessed them to be Chippendales. Huge, ornate mirrors decorated the walls.

Login Lurch turned to lecture them. "There will be no smoking, or partying," he said in his deep voice. "However, there are sandwich materials and wines in the kitchen. I do not reside here as does no one else, so you will be here alone."

He looked almost gleeful at the thought.

"In the morning you will find breakfast in the..."

he paused and pointed to a door to his right, "...breakfast room. You have two rooms on the ground floor. You will be on the ground floor due to," and he paused again and actually smiled. "Your age."

They looked at each other. Marge and Hadley did eye rolls.

"Must have watched you come up the stairs," Robbie whispered to Marge.

Marge just gripped her cane tighter and wondered if they would find Uncle Fester Addams in residence on the top floor.

Login led them to their rooms, opened the door to each and smiled the most horrendous smile any of them had ever seen. He was obviously pleased about something.

"This room was Madam Romanov's, the first generation here," he said, standing at the door to Marge and Mary Rose's room. "It was here that she murdered herself."

"Oh, my gosh," Mary Rose said. "She completed suicide right here?"

"Oh no, Mum," Login said. "Madam hated herself. It was clearly murder."

Robbie remembered those lines. He's seen the *Murder by Death*, movie, she thought.

He left, and Marge thought she heard him chuckle, but it might just have been his teeth knocking together.

They settled into rooms that were nothing less than elegant: two canopied beds in each room, a fireplace with wood and fire starters, antique tables and chairs, expensive antique braided rugs and even more expensive bedding. Mary Rose and Marge's room had a beautiful, small love seat and Hadley and Robbie's room had a black leather fainting couch.

There were no closets, as was common in houses of this age, but two big wardrobes were against the wall on each side of the beds. There were two matching luggage racks open and waiting for their suitcases, and the wood on luggage racks, chairs and beds was burled walnut.

"You can't buy this kind of wood anymore," Hadley said loudly from across the hall.

The hallway was wide, the walls adorned with family portraits and more mirrors. Exquisite Persian runners graced the floor. From their doors they could see the entryway to the mansion and the huge bouquet of fresh flowers on the table inside.

"Lots of money in here," Hadley said.

They put their clothes away, Geoffrey found a spot on the rug that suited him, and they all lay down, covered up with the beautiful soft afghans they found gracefully folded at the foot of the beds. They took a well-deserved nap.

"Naps used to be a luxury," Marge said when they met late in the afternoon in the hallway. "Now they're a necessity."

It was getting dark, as it does early in Alaska in the spring. They found the kitchen and looked around. It was, as expected, antique but well done. There was a modern dishwasher and state-of-the-art stove. There was a huge, round, oak, claw-foot table with matching chairs that could easily seat twelve. One wall was entirely made up of large windows.

Marge hung the red cane over one chair and claimed it for her own.

The contents of the refrigerator did not disappoint. There was ham and beef and cheese and one totally unidentified meat along with various fruit salads, vegetable salads and breads.

“Not bad,” Marge said. They agreed, and Hadley popped open a bottle of champagne, one of four nestled into the refrigerator.

“We haven’t paid the Lurch man yet,” Mary Rose said.

“I’ll leave some cash on the table if we don’t see him again,” Hadley said.

“I’m guessing it will be around seventy-five dollars,” Marge offered.

“I’ll leave a hundred and fifty cash in case,” Hadley volunteered.

They found games in a cupboard in the kitchen and settled around the table for their favorite; Monopoly. By ten o’clock Mary Rose had done it again by getting hotels on the entire north and east sides of the board, and they were all ready to go to sleep.

Geoffrey was outfitted with a bowl for water and had enjoyed his own sandwiches. He was unusually restless, though, and every so often he would whine a soft, pitiful whine.

“New places,” Marge observed, patting him gently.

They nodded and each one gave the big dog a pat or hug.

He still whined.

The first gigantic flash of lightning, followed by a spectacular clap of thunder came as they reached their rooms. It was followed by a second tremendous flash of lightning and another roll of thunder.

“Holy moly!” Robbie said.

“Open the front door,” Mary Rose said. “See if there is really a storm is or if we’re stuck with a ghost again.”

Robbie hurried to the front door, opened it, and was drenched when the wind blew the rain full blast into the entrance.

“It’s a real storm!” she yelled, wiping her face on her damp sleeve.

Rain hammered against the windows. The whole

house shook with dangerous gusts of wind. By the time they were dressed for bed and under the covers they could hear sleet pounding on walls and windows.

A shutter came loose and banged.

Geoffrey made one Olympic-quality jump and landed in bed with Mary Rose. He was trembling as he snuggled in beside her. She put her arm around him and held him right. "It's okay, Geoff. It's okay."

"Are you saying that to him or yourself," Marge smiled.

"Yes," Mary Rose smiled back.

It was just as they began to doze off that the laughter began.

From somewhere in the house, they could hear a wicked, high-pitched woman's voice, laughing a mean, inhuman laugh.

Geoffrey lifted his head, growled and whined. Mary Rose hurried to her feet. "I'm going across the hall, Marge. Come on, let's all be together."

She grabbed pillows and blankets, Marge grabbed her red cane, and both women hurried into the hallway. Coming out of the room across the hall were Hadley and Robbie, each carrying pillows and blankets and headed to Marge and Mary Rose's room.

They met in the middle of the hall.

"Did you hear the laughter?" Robbie asked.

The big house was totally silent.

Marge and Mary Rose nodded.

"Well," Marge said, taking control, "your room has the fainting couch. Mary Rose and I can take turns trying to sleep there."

"We'll share our beds with you like big girls," Hadley said, "but do we need to find who is laughing?"

As soon as she asked, she shook her head. They were all shaking their heads.

"Answer is, 'Nope'," Hadley said, and she turned and led the way into the room with the fainting couch.

The Fainting Couch

They stood for a moment once they got inside the room, as if waiting for the laughter to echo through the mansion again.

Nothing.

It was Mary Rose who began to laugh. "Just look at us," and she pointed to each of them. "We're beautiful, beautiful, beautiful!"

Marge was wearing a pair of black satin pajamas with fuzzy black slippers on her feet. Hadley had on a white negligee with lace trim and had three rollers in her hair. Robbie had her favorite sleep shirt which pictured a bear holding a garden trowel and a flower in a pot and the words, 'Hairy Potter'. Her own little bear was tucked under her arm, and Mary Rose had on a long, pink flannel nightgown.

"Beautiful, beautiful, beautiful!" they said together.

Then they heard the laughter one more time.

"I don't have a clue what it is or who it is," Marge said. "Let's say the Lurch guy left a laugh record on or something."

"Login," Hadley corrected.

"I'm going to try the fainting couch," Mary Rose said. She patted Geoffrey. "I know Puppers here will want to come up with me and there's room."

Geoffrey was staying close beside Mary Rose and continued to whine and tremble now and then.

The fainting couch was done in a beautiful black leather with the back of one end raised and edged with the same exquisite burl walnut as the other furniture. Popular in the nineteenth century, the couches were mainly for women whose corsets were so tight the ladies became, well...faint. They were also used for what was called "female hysteria" and since only one end had a back, the couches could accommodate the large hoop skirts fashionable in Victorian times.

Mary Rose sat down, put a pillow behind her head, draped a blanket over herself, tucking it around her feet, leaned back and patted the area beside her for Geoffrey.

Geoffrey was relieved.

He took a running jump, lept onto the couch, and as he sat on Mary Rose, the entire piece of furniture fell over on its side with a loud crash.

"Mary Rose!" Hadley yelled. "You okay?"

The pillow and blanket were over Mary Rose's head.

"mimm fiinne," she mumbled through the bedding, and she began to untangle herself.

Sensing that this wasn't going to be an extended play, and not feeling up to it himself, Geoffrey came to his lady and licked her face as soon as it appeared from under the blanket and pillow.

"Oh drat," Marge said, looking at the back of the couch. "Geoff's nails must have made a little tear here."

She reached down and pulled a small piece of ripped fabric back into place. "It's fixable," she said.

She was quiet for a minute.

They watched and waited. She obviously had her hand through the tear, feeling around inside the couch.

"Son of a gun!" she said under her breath. "Hadley, you know what these are?"

She handed a handful of gems to Hadley.

"Again," Hadley said. "Sapphires and rubies and I'm guessing there's a little diamond here as well."

"The first clue on the map," Marge said. "All those places on the map must have jewels hidden somewhere."

"When I was Googling Gospel Bird," Robbie said, "there were stories about the Romanov family hiding their jewels in Gospel Bird, but the webpages always mentioned the rumors about the mines and caves that surround the town."

They were quiet, looking at the handful of jewels.

All was silent in the mansion as well.

That's when the lights went out.

They put on their bathrobes and slippers, Marge's being the biggest and blackest, and stood huddled together in the dark in Hadley and Robbie's room, Hadley slipped the jewels into one pocket of her robe and pulled out her cell phone from the other pocket.

She turned it on and tapped the flashlight. A soft light surrounded them.

“My eyes take so dang long to adjust to the dark with this Macular Degeneration!” she complained.

“They’re not adjusting, girlfriend,” Marge said. “It’s that dark.”

There was no light at all.

The clouds were low and heavy.

Ominous rumbles of thunder followed flashes of lightning in the distance. When one flash lit the room for a second, the girls headed for the door, led by Marge.

“We’ll see if the lights are out all over the house,” she said.

As if they were on anywhere.

The other three turned on their flashlights and hurried into the hall, their phones providing a good light.

“Dang again!” Hadley said. “My battery just died.” Her light went off.

"Oh, crap!" Robbie said. "Now mine's gone."

"It's okay," Marge said, "we really only need one and we still have two." She had, entirely out of good habit, grabbed her cane and was holding onto it with a tight grip.

Hadley felt along the wall until she came to a light switch.

No luck.

The power was definitely out everywhere.

Geoffrey was still huddling, this time between Mary Rose and Robbie. Then Mary Rose felt him move. At the same time, footsteps sounded down the hall near the kitchen door.

"Hello!" Marge called. "Is that you, Login?"

The footsteps hurried on.

Geoffrey made a surprise move. He hurried around to be in front of the four friends, between them and the heavy footsteps. He went into a mean-looking crouch and began to growl. It wasn't Geoffrey's usual wimpy growl-whine combination. This growl meant business. Those legs were ready to spring. As they watched him,

Marge's light settled on the hall in front of the kitchen. Mary Rose aimed her light on the big dog. Geoffrey's growl changed. A definite snarl, filled with warning and courage took over.

Geoffrey wasn't going to let anything hurt his ladies.

"I don't think anything is going to get past our dog," Robbie said.

"If anyone wants to hurt us," Mary Rose added, "they have to come through our protector."

"Good dog, Geoff," Robbie said.

"Quiet," Marge ordered.

They were quiet.

So was the mansion.

So was the night.

The footsteps had stopped.

"Are we going to go see who it is if they're in the kitchen?" Mary Rose asked.

"Ask the guard dog," Marge replied.

Geoffrey was still on point, even though mastiffs don't point.

He was ready to attack.

"I don't think so," Hadley said. "Let's go back, lock our door and try to get some sleep."

"Hah!" Robbie said. Sleep did not seem like even a remote possibility.

They backed up toward the room. When they were part way there, Geoffrey spun around, whined once and was the first one through the door.

Bravery can't last forever.

Robbie lit a fire in the fireplace, Marge looked at her phone and announced it was nearly one in the morning, and Geoffrey unexpectedly lay down directly in front of the door. If anyone tried to get in, they would have to move one hundred seventy-five pounds of muscle that was not only close to the ground, but on the ground.

"Sometimes he just surprises me," Mary Rose said.

It was obvious that the big mastiff was not going to sleep.

But the girls did.

When Mary Rose woke up, the sky was still cloudy, and the rain had stopped. Geoffrey was still in front of the door, watching her. She reached for her phone and saw it was nearly nine o'clock.

"I know you have to go out," she whispered.

Geoffrey's tail thumped once, and he stood up.

She slipped on her robe and slippers, snapped on Geoffrey's leash and began to lead him out into the hall.

All was quiet.

A soft, hazy light came in through the large, heavily-draped windows.

Geoffrey, who was carefully trained not to pull when on his leash, pulled - just a little - toward the closed kitchen door behind which the laughter had issued with an eerie shrill.

He put his nose to the beautiful, decorative, shiny hardwood floor, sniffing its wide planks and running his nose under the closed kitchen door.

He whined softly, backed up, looked at Mary Rose and grinned.

"Good dog, good Geoffrey," Mary Rose said, and they went out the front door into an even more hazy, cool Alaskan morning. Mary Rose hadn't thought to grab her jacket, so she wrapped her robe righter and held it around her shoulders.

Geoffrey didn't take long. When they hurried back in, he looked at the kitchen door but didn't stop to investigate.

Mary Rose breathed a sigh of relief and scurried into the room she had intended to share with Marge. She could hear the water running, and knew Marge was in the shower. A well-decorated bathroom was part of each room and theirs had an antique sink and an old toilet with the porcelain reservoir hung on the wall above it. A gold chain with a crystal ball on the end served as the flush handle. The shower was small but comfortable, with a glass door and bright, recessed lighting,

It was indeed, a fine old mansion.

As promised by Login, an equally elegant breakfast of scones, rye breads, jellies, fruits and three different types of sausage was laid out in a room near the kitchen. Sweet buns with raisins were on a big plate, in the center of which was a smaller bouquet of fresh flowers.

It was indeed, a fine Russian breakfast.

The breakfast room itself was in bright yellow colors with a yellow table, yellow chairs, yellow pillows and the great windows draped with soft, yellow curtains.

"Lots of yellow here," Marge said, putting her red cane on the largest yellow chair.

Hadley looked thoughtful. "We're here alone," she almost whispered. "Let's search the house. Let's explore all three floors."

Their eyes brightened.

In just minutes, the four friends had found a small elevator, big enough for only two people at a time, at the far end of the hall. Two-by-two, they went up to the third floor.

They stepped out and looked around in another long hallway.

Hadley looked at the ceiling, 'There's got to be an entrance to that widow's walk on the roof," she said.

They found it, pulled hard to get a set of stairs to lower in front of them, then climbed up - carefully - and stood on the stairs, Hadley on the top step. Geoffrey whined and stayed behind.

Hadley pushed hard on a trap door in the ceiling above her.

"Locked," she said.

"We should have sent you up alone," Marge complained, favoring her knee as she backed down.

There were more bedrooms, a storage room filled with stacks of what looked like priceless art leaning against and hanging on the walls.

Robbie looked at some of the pictures. "Do you know that the greatest art collection in the world was owned by Catherine the Great of Russia? Art dealers, who dealt in the finest old painters' work would travel Europe and end up in Russia, where they knew Catherine would buy everything they had left."

"I read where she had chairs that were carved with human figures having sex," Hadley added, holding up a small pastoral painting and looking on the back of it.

"My kind of girl, that Catherine," Marge added.

"Who would want something like that?" Mary Rose asked.

"Catherine the Great," they said together.

The second floor had a room in which coffee and teas were served and more bedrooms, all with canopied beds, ornate bathrooms and expensive rugs on even more expensive floors.

Mary Rose checked her hair in a mirror in every room. "I've GOT to see Peyton when I get home, my hair is out of control."

She was right.

"Why would Login put us on the first floor, as he said, 'because of our age,' when there's an elevator we could take to the two top floors?" Hadley asked.

"So we would hear the laughter," Marge said.

They were quiet for a few minutes then, still without speaking, they took the elevator back down to the main floor.

In all their snooping and feeling they weren't dirty or dusty. The entire mansion was spotless. "Login is a good housekeeper," Hadley said.

"Wonder if he does interiors of Hummers," Robbie said.

Mary Rose noticed a beautiful, embroidered bell pull hanging on the wall near the breakfast room door.

"Oh girls! Remember the bell pull in Christmas Carol, how it rang just before Marley's ghost appeared?"

She gave a playful yank on the beautiful pull that hung from the ceiling to her shoulder.

The same gong that served as the doorbell banged again,

Everyone, including Geoffrey, jumped.

Suddenly, standing beside them, seeming to materialize out of thin air instead of coming through a door like normal humans, stood Login the butler.

"You rang?" He asked.

They were all quiet, then Hadley spoke up. “We want to pay you for last night, Login. We don’t think we’ll need another night.”

He motioned Hadley to a Chippendale desk against one wall.

Mary Rose and Geoffrey, who obviously did not like Login, went to a window and looked out.

“Robbie,” Mary Rose said softly. She smiled and pointed out the window.

Robbie hurried to her side, looked out and grinned from ear to ear.

The Hummer and Alphonso’s van had pulled up in the circle drive. Stepping out of the driver’s seat in the Hummer was a tall, muscular Indian. He was dressed in black boots, black slacks, a black turtleneck and a black jacket with an Apache Security patch on one shoulder. Around his neck was a gold chain with one inlaid turquoise stone, and on the middle finger of his right hand was a large, multi-jeweled Indian ring. His hair, with long grey streaks, was in a single braid that hung below his shoulders.

“Raven!” Robbie said under her breath.

And she hurried out the door and into his arms, her little bear still clutched tightly against her chest, Geoffrey passing her on the porch and reaching his hero first.

Geoffrey loved Raven. The big Indian had never had to train or even talk to the dog. Geoffrey just went immediately to heel and would die for Raven, just as he would lose his own life for his ladies.

Denali

The men ate hearty breakfasts, and the women drank coffee and munched on potato skin appetizers. They had eaten well at Wander Lost. Waitress was flirting with Raven and winking at the girls and the Ill Eagle was as comfortable and welcoming as usual. Robbie sat next to Raven and refused to take her hand off his knee.

“How was the B&B?” Wiley asked, looking at the girls in general. “You look like you didn’t have the best night’s sleep.”

“Nonsense!” Mary Rose said, “We’re beautiful.”

“Beautiful, beautiful, beautiful,” Marge echoed.

“It was great,” Hadley said.

“It was elegant,” Robbie added.

They looked at each other, grinned and Hadley leaned forward. “You won’t believe what happened!” And they began their story of the Haunting at Wander Lost and a hidden packet of jewels.

Hadley reached into her purse, brought out the jewels in a little cloth packet where she had carefully secured them, and spread them out on the table.

"Wow!" Wiley said.

"Well, I'll be," Alphonso said.

Raven said nothing, but his eyes got just a little wider.

"There are more jewels on that map," Hadley pointed out. "We're sure of it. We just have to find them."

"Once you find them, what will you do with them?" Wiley asked.

They looked at him.

"We'll think of something," Marge said.

Waitress came out of the kitchen with coffee pots for refills and Hadley swooped up the jewels and quickly put them away.

As he looked up at Waitress, Alphonso noticed a tall, skinny man standing at a table near them, looking directly at where the jewels had been.

"Uh oh," he said under his breath. He reached

down and pinched Wiley's arm and nodded at the skinny man. Wiley looked and nodded back.

The man at the other table turned immediately and hurried out the door. He was wearing an Indian parka, a black beat-up hat with a wide brim and what looked like genuine Muk-luk boots, the soft boots worn by Eskimos in the Arctic, lined with fur and made from Sealskin or Reindeer hide.

Robbie noticed him earlier because she had always wanted a pair of Muk-luks and could never afford them.

"Didn't notice him until he stood up and looked at the jewels," Alphonso said after telling the girls what he and Wiley had seen.

"He followed us from the bed and breakfast," Raven said, taking a long sip of his coffee.

"How do you see all those things?" Mary Rose asked in a surprised voice.

"Apache Indian trick," Raven answered. And he squeezed Robbie's hand.

"I wish to go someplace," Raven announced. "I need to do a meditation before I meet Ms. Bushwhacker."

Marge didn't think anyone had ever called her cousin "Ms." before.

"I have spoken by phone with the Judge and am officially Ms. Bushwhacker's defense attorney. I understand the Judge is called Judge Judge. It is a wise father who names his children what he wishes them to become. He looked at Robinson Leary and smiled. "You, Robbie, steal hearts, just as the great Jackie Robinson stole bases. Your name fits you."

"Yeah, well mine sounds like margarine," Marge Aaron said, smiling.

"Then you 'butter' be good," Alphonso teased.

"I wish to go to the sacred mountain, Denali," Raven continued. "There is a train we can catch from Gospel Bird, spend a delightful night in the lodge there," he squeezed Robbie's hand again. She blushed. "and enjoy the beauty while I do a short meditation."

"How do we go about that?" Hadley asked. "Where is the railroad station? We've seen most of Gospel Bird and I don't remember finding it."

"The arrangements are already made," Raven said. "The station is in the center of the town, disguised as city hall." He looked at his watch which rested in a large turquoise band. "We leave in two hours."

"Geoffrey?" Mary Rose asked.

"Convinced them," Raven smiled.

Mary Rose looked at Marge. "More Apache Indian tricks?"

Gretchen and Bullwinkle

The train was comfortable for everyone except Geoffrey.

He was cramped into a small compartment and left alone with only a blanket, water bowl and a small cardboard-like wall built across what looked like the center of the tiny room.

He snorted. Humans.

He was ready to lay down and ignore the world when the train started with a sizeable jerk, then another. He caught his balance and wuffed. To his surprise, his "wuff" was answered by a soft whine that came from the other side of the flimsy wall.

The train began to move, and so did Geoffrey.

He turned and put his forehead against the wall.

"Wuff!"

"Smerff, smerff, wuff," came a response.

Geoffrey's ears went up, his tail sprung straight into the air and he sniffed a long, delicious sniff.

Dog!

Girl dog!

Girl dog who smelled wonderful.

Geoffrey pushed hard against the cardboard wall.

The soft whine came again from the other side.

Geoffrey pushed harder.

It sounded as if the dog on the other side was clawing at the bottom of the wall. They were working together for freedom.

After a few minutes, the wall began to give. It moved an inch, bent, slid and came down with a muffled bang and landed on the dog on the other side.

Uh oh.

Geoffrey sniffed, waited and held his breath.

Then the remains of the wall started to move. Pushing and shoving the splintered fake wood was the most beautiful golden retriever he had ever seen. She made the most glamorous poodle took like an ugly mixed breed. And she had been groomed! Her coat was perfect, her eyes were deep and dark, and he was sure she had eyelashes that were at least three inches long.

And her tail!

Her tail was perfect, her legs divine, and she was big. Geoffrey liked big.

If there had been music, a string quartet would be in the little compartment playing that classic tune that is always there when lovers run across the beach and jump into each other's arms. At the very least, a piano would be rendering the theme from, "Lady and the Tramp."

"Oh, great god of dogs," Geoffrey thought as best he could. "I wish I hadn't been neutered!"

Her wide pink collar had, "Gretchen" on it in silver studs.

To Geoffrey it looked like 6&*#+%#$ but it didn't matter.

Gretchen looked at Geoffrey, opened her beautiful mouth that framed her great teeth and grinned a big doggie grin.

Geoffrey fell over on his back, opened his own mouth, grinned back and looked at her upside down.

She lowered her head and nuzzled his chest.

His heart was about to leave his body.

His doggie soul was getting a look at Heaven.

Then the train came to a sudden stop and Gretchen the Golden, fell forward right onto Geoffrey.

He began to lick her gorgeous face and they looked into each other's big, brown, doggie eyes. Romance.

In their own compartment, the friends looked out the window to see a small station and a few passengers waiting to board the train. Everyone was looking at something in front of the engine. Several were pointing and laughing.

"Something funny out there," Hadley said.

"Let's go look," Mary Rose said. "I need to stretch. My back is starting to hurt."

There was something funny alright. As Robbie looked out her window, she looked directly at the protective lattice work that did its best to keep the strong north and west winds away from the station's door. There was a good fifteen inches open above the ground, put there she imagined, to keep the drifts from piling up along the side.

As she looked, she saw a pair of Muk-Luks dashing through the open area and disappearing through the door and into the station.

She looked at Raven, sitting by her side. He was looking out the window as well. He looked back at her and nodded.

They all stood up, piled out and walked to the front of the train.

"Be leaving in a few," the conductor said.

"What's out there that's so interesting?" Marge asked.

"Bullwinkle the Moose," the conductor smiled. "The guys here at the station found him when he was just a day or so old, raised him and now that he's a teenager, he still hangs around. He knows to the minute the times this train is coming and going. He gets on the tracks and doesn't move until he gets his treat."

"His treat?" Robbie asked.

"A peanut butter sandwich with butter and cream cheese," the conductor said.

"Sounds kind of good," Wiley said to Alphonso and Raven. They nodded.

"Aren't they dangerous?" Mary Rose asked.

"The moose or the station guys?" the conductor grinned.

Robbie broke in. "I understood that the best way to treat a moose was to avoid them entirely."

"True," the conductor said. He was an older gentleman with a neat mustache and an old-fashioned conductor's uniform. It looked good on him.

They all went down the steps to see Bullwinkle, who was, as the conductor said, standing in the center of the tracks blocking any movement the train might make.

Bullwinkle was as expected, a young moose. His long, spindly legs looked tremendously awkward, his antlers were getting a good start and his nose was exceptionally long.

"He's got to grow into that nose," Alphonso said.

They waited.

And waited.

As they watched, three different men came out of the station with Bullwinkle's sandwiches. The first man gave him the sandwich, made strange motions for him to leave, waited then turned and walked back to the station. The second man did the same thing with a new sandwich. He waited even longer. Then the third sandwich man appeared with the treat and he, too, made strange, unaccountable motions for Bullwinkle to move.

He didn't.

This went on for at least twenty minutes. The conductor looked at his watch more than once.

"He's not moving," one of the rail workers said.

"Keen sense of the obvious," Wiley said.

"I'm ready to get on our way," Marge said, and she took ahold of the handle of her cane and started to carefully walk down the track toward the moose.

“Wouldn’t Apache Indian tricks be better right now?” Mary Rose asked, looking desperately at Raven.

“Apaches do not bother the moose,” Raven answered.

“Moose smarter?’ Alphonso asked.

Raven laughed, “I’ll put my money on Marge in this one.”

The conductor kept yelling, “Ma’am! Ma’am!”

Marge didn’t stop. By the time the three rail workers started toward her, she was eye-to-eye with Bullwinkle.

They stared at each other.

The rail workers stopped in their tracks.

Marge raised her cane.

“She’s not going to Taser him!” Mary Rose said, loudly.

Everyone looked at Mary Rose, then shot their stares back to Marge and the moose.

Bullwinkle stared at her, too.

Marge raised her cane, gently popped Bullwinkle on his long nose, and the distinguished homicide detective let out a squeak that sounded exactly like one of the squeaky toys Geoffrey devoured now and then.

Bop! EEEEEEEP!!

The moose looked at her, gave a soft EEEP in return, shook his head, looked at her again, snorted, paused for a second then quickly turned and walked with his awkward teenage walk into the woods next to the railroad track.

The passengers applauded.

"I think he did an eye roll," Hadley said.

Marge almost strutted back to them, a satisfied grin on her face.

"Retired homicide detective trick," Marge said as Raven took her arm, gave her a little boost, and she pulled herself up the stairs and boarded the train.

When they arrived in Denali, they found Geoffrey and Gretchen, curled up together, sound asleep. His paw was over her paw and their cheeks were touching.

Puppy love.

But it couldn't last.

A pretty woman with white hair and wearing a long red coat, red gloves and red boots claimed Gretchen when the train stopped. The lady took off her red gloves and rubbed Gretchen's neck while both Gretchen and Geoffrey tried to tell her they wanted to be together.

The lady snapped a long, pink leash on Gretchen, patted her and began to lead her down the hall toward the steps under the "exit" sign. Steps that would take her away forever.

Gretchen twisted around and looked at Geoffrey. She looked longingly at him all the way down the long, narrow train hallway.

Geoffrey watched through the open door and felt sadder then he had ever felt before.

Is it really better to have loved and lost than to not have loved at all?

At the moment, he wasn't sure.

The friends enjoyed the tallest mountain in North America. Denali was beautiful.

They had a wonderful evening and night together. Robbie and Raven had their own room in the classy lodge, Mary Rose and Wiley were in the room next door, Alphonso and Marge were down the hall and Hadley and a new James Hankins book were in a large room on the top floor.

She thought about the fact that everyone else was with someone special, making love and snuggling together, but she didn't mind. She spent some time thinking about the two men whom she had loved and how lucky she was to have known them and given them her heart. Her husband and Wes Longbow were all she needed. She opened a small bottle of white wine from the room's refrigerator and settled in with her tablet and wine in a real glass. She fell asleep before she finished the wine.

"So, when did he leave?" Mary Rose asked Robbie.

They met at the departure point for the park buses that would take them, and a lot of other tourists, on a six-hour tour of Denali National Park. Tucked into Mary Rose's bag were muffins for breakfast and sandwiches and soft drinks for lunch. It was a sunny day, and there was just a kiss of a breeze blowing across the big patio that led to the buses. At least fifty other tourists were waiting with them.

"I don't know," Robbie answered. "He was gone when I woke up. I have no idea where he went."

"Went to find his center," Alphonso answered as he did his best to saunter up to them using his two canes. "Went to get into his zone. Used to do that before games. He'd meditate, get all quiet, then he'd quietly come out and kill us all. When we see him again, he'll be ready to defend Buckshot Betsy and do away with the prosecutor." Alphonso laughed with memories, then seemed to drift off into his own zone. "Chuck Benarik tackled Frank Gifford, head to shoulder in 1960, legal hit, and took Gifford out for over a year." He shook his head and smiled. "That's how Raven will defend Betsy. Adios, Mr. Prosecutor."

They did the tourist thing - bus ride, actually seeing bears and elk and mountain sheep. They paid a visit to the dogs that patrolled the park with dog sleds, did shopping at the gift shops and precisely at 5pm, they got Geoffrey from the doggie kennel where he had spent an entire day pouting and trying to remember Gretchen. Still sad, he rode with them when they took a bus to the rail station.

Raven was waiting for them.

He hugged Robbie, nodded a knowing nod at Alphonso, and announced that he wanted to visit Buckshot Betsy's cabin the next day. He didn't look as if he was planning on killing anybody, despite what Alphonso said.

Bullwinkle the Moose was not at the little station as the train made its stop there, nor was anyone wearing Muk-luks.

The Cabin

Geoffrey was still sad the next day, but his doggie brain was beginning to forget why. Like many of us who grieve, only a gentle good memory remained; a memory of a beautiful golden dog with a pink collar licking his face and chest.

He was with his people. Life was good again, and he was going Ride.

Raven drove the Hummer up the steep incline toward Buckshot Betsy's cabin, which was located on a mountainside near Gospel Bird.

Marge had talked to her cousin three times since they last saw her and each time Manley the sheriff complained and told her not to call again. Each time Marge threatened him with her lawyer. Once she said, "If you google my lawyer's name, what comes up is 'meanest SOB in the valley - I do not fear your valley of death because MY lawyer is the meanest..." she got that far, and Betsy was on the line.

Her spirits were bright. She had not met Raven but trusted her cousin and during their last conversation was enjoying a winning hand in bridge.

It took almost an hour to get to Betsy's home. The cabin was made of beautiful logs, carefully placed together. A small shed graced the back and was nestled into the woods so that it looked picturesque. Geoffrey bounced toward the shed to sniff and investigate.

There was a monster stack of firewood in a big wood holder a few feet from the cabin door. Betsy, tall as she was, could probably reach out in the worst blizzard, grab a chunk of firewood and never leave her cabin.

There was only one room, with a partition that bordered off a tiny toilet and sink. There had to be a septic tank outside.

"Sponge bath city," Marge commented.

"What more do you need?" Wiley asked.

A large hand-braided rug covered the floor. A comfortable-looking bed was tucked into a corner next to a window. There was a beautiful, colorful quilt on the bed and another quilt covering a north window. That quilt served as both classy wall décor and a window blanket from the north wind. There were antique chairs, a small table, an old wooden trunk, a small closet and some not-half-bad artwork hung tastefully on the remaining walls.

There was also a shattered door.

Raven spent a long time looking at the door.

He had Alphonso stand where Betsy would have stood. Raven stood outside. Wiley stood outside. Hadley stood outside. Raven measured.

Geoffrey finished his exploring, peed on the woodpile and trotted inside to lay down.

Wiley found the Bear Killer, Betsy's big rifle and admired it. "Oldie but goodie," he said.

Raven checked to see if it was loaded.

Along the wall next to the fireplace was a series of beautifully carved shelves. Betsy had various knick-knacks and books arranged on them.

Mary Rose walked over to the shelves and took down a sweet pair of salt and pepper shakers.

"Look," she said to the girls. "It's a Gingham Dog and Calico Cat." She cradled the little shakers in her hand. They were unusually heavy.

She shook the Calico Cat.
It rattled.

She shook it again.

“The salt has been in her so long it’s gotten hard,” she said.

She shook it again.

“Wait a minute,” Hadley said, taking the Calico Cat from Mary Rose.

Hadley shook it.

“That’s too hard for calcified salt,” Hadley said.

They gathered around.

Hadley tried to take the little stopper out of the shaker but it wouldn’t loosen.

Raven tried.

The stopper was there to stay.

“Sorry, Buckshot,” Raven said, and he threw the little shaker on the floor where it broke into two big pieces.

Tumbling out of it were four rubies and one diamond.

“It’s glue-able,” Mary Rose said, picking up the broken pieces.

“More jewels,” Robbie said, picking up the gems that had escaped onto the floor.

“The plot thickens,” Alphonso said.

Raven, without a word, turned and walked out the door.

Geoffrey was the first one out after him, and on the way to the shed he managed a second small pee on the stack of wood.

They followed him to the little shed in back and watched as he, as carefully as possible, pulled the locked door off the shed.

“Muscles,” Hadley whispered to Robbie.

“Oh, yes,” Robbie whispered back.

“Apache Indian trick,” Marge whispered from behind them.

It was dark inside the shed, but they could see an old dog sled, garden tools and three broken chairs. There were two boxes, carefully packed and taped shut.

"Open," Raven said, pointing to the boxes.

Wiley took out his knife and tore the tape open on the boxes. They were full of old photos.

Marge sat on the one broken chair that would hold her, and started to look through the pictures.

"Here are my parents!" she smiled.

The girls gathered around to look at the pictures Marge was pulling out.

Wiley went over to the old dog sled and got behind the handles. "Mush!" he yelled.

"Try 'Steak'!'" Alphonso laughed. "No smart dog goes for mush anymore."

Geoffrey heard, 'smart dog' and looked at Alphonso.

Wiley yelled, "Steak, you huskies," and pulled on the handles.

They both broke off with a dull crack.

Wiley looked shocked.

Then they all looked shocked.

Rolling onto the floor under the sled were more jewels, many of which even Hadley did not recognize. A good section of the floor was covered with them after they tumbled out of the sled's handles.

There were a few seconds of stunned silence then -

"You might try the real words we use," came a voice from the door. "Hike! Gee! Haw! And if you're lucky, 'Trail! or On By!' That one means you're going to pass the sled ahead of you."

Standing in the door was a tall, attractive older gentleman in a red parka. He had a pleasant smile and because he had a cane, he seemed to fit right in.

"I see you found some of the jewels," he smiled.

There was nothing threatening or mean-looking about him and he was not wearing Muk-luks.

Musher, Mayor and Historian - Kind of

The man stepped through the door, the sun playing off his white hair. “Mark Merrill,” he said, introducing himself and taking a step toward Raven. His smile was pleasant, and he held out his hand. “I believe you’re Betsy’s attorney.” Raven shook hands and introduced everyone.

“I check on Betsy every so often and she keeps track of me. We’re kind of neighbors.” He motioned with his head toward the mountain. “I’ve watched the cabin while she’s been in jail. How’s it looking for her, Counselor?”

Raven smiled a soft smile. “It should never have come to trial. It was clearly an accident.”

“Well, it won’t take much to make Sheriff Manley Malaprop look like the idiot he is,” Mark said. “And as for Slik Quick - don’t turn your back on him. He looks dumb, and in some ways he is, but he pulls rabbits out of hats now and then in his spare time.” He paused. “Then he eats them.”

“What about Judge Jonkers?” Raven asked.

"Judge Judge Jonkers," Mark said, and Robbie did an eye roll at the mention of the name. "Not a bad man and he's fair. He obviously hasn't read everything yet or he'd probably throw the case out for lack of cause."

"Good to know," Raven said.

Mark Merrill looked around the shed and obviously made a judgment about each of the friends. "I'm a past mayor of Gospel Bird," he said. "I'm kind of a racer. I ran dogs in the Iditarod for four years - Betsy helped me train 'em, and I'm also kind of the local historian." He smiled. "Sounds like I have a lot of kind of in my life, don't I?"

"I'd like to hear from the kind of historian, about the jewels," Alphonso said.

"And I'd kind of like an Iditarod story," Wiley added.

Mary Rose took a step forward, "Mr. Merrill, "do you happen to know where I can find an Inukshuk?"

The Legend of the Romanov Jewels

The kind of historian turned and headed toward the door. "Meet you in an hour at the sick bird."

They looked at each other.

He stopped.

"The Ill Eagle restaurant," he said as he walked out into the sunlight. They could hear him chuckle a soft chuckle.

"The story goes, and mind you it IS just a story, that the descendants of Czar Nicholas II came to America after the revolution in 1917 and settled in the area around Gospel Bird." Mark Merrill was holding his steaming cup of hot coffee between his hands at a table in the center of The Ill Eagle.

No other customers were around on this pleasant mid-afternoon. The bartender was polishing glasses behind the huge, ornate bar, earplugs blasting music into his brain. If they wanted anything they either went to the bar or waved frantically. They didn't need anything. Each one had a big mug of coffee and the barkeep had placed a huge bowl of popcorn in the center of the table. Mary Rose thought how nice it would be, once they got back to Omaha, to settle in with popcorn with goldfish crackers and M&Ms and a glass of champagne, their usual movie treats.

Merrill continued, "Our Romanov family ruled Russia for 100 years and that ended in 1917 amidst a civil war, a world war and a bloody revolution. Czars ruled Russia for 300 years. During that time they established what was called, 'The Diamond Fund,' which meant they had more crown jewels than you can imagine."

"They must have had all the riches Catherine the Great collected," Robbie added. She was soaking this up like a 150-pound sponge.

"Probably," Mark went on. "We know some of the story of the most valuable jewels in history because of a man who worked for Tiffany's. George Frederick Kunz traveled all over Russia in carriages in 1890. He wrote that he always had a gun across his knees because he didn't trust his driver. Anyway, he was on a mission to find 'the peasant queen of amethysts' and," here he looked up and smiled at Robbie, "his writings are still available."

Mark took a sip of his coffee. "The University of St Petersburg convinced the Bolsheviks to keep the jewels as historical treasures instead of selling them. The Revolution, called Red October..."

"Red October. Like the movie about the submarine," Wiley interrupted.

"Starring Sean Connery," Mary Rose added.

"Hollywood romanced a lot of it," Robbie said. "There are movies about Rasputin and Anastasia and the revolution, of course."

Mark nodded. "Yes, the Red October boys were hard to convince because they needed money, but they came around and now the crown jewels are on display at the Kremlin in Moscow."

"They toured the US in 1995," Hadley broke in, "I saw them in New York."

"They did, indeed," Mark nodded. "But as for the smaller jewels, the ones like you all found, that's where the legend of Gospel Bird begins and the questions multiply. Are they the real jewels from The Diamond Fund? Who brought them here? Are there only small ones or are some of the ones like the bracelets or brooches or even the jewels from the Czar's scepter hidden in the mines or caves in the mountains where most people have searched for years?"

He stopped for a dramatic pause.

"Nobody knows," he finished.

They were quiet for a minute, then Wiley remembered something.

"We heard the joke about men crouched in corners giving themselves estrogen shots when Susan Butcher kept winning the Iditarod so many times in a row," Wiley said. "You ran that race you said."

"I did. And it's a race to beat all races. The biggest event in Alaska runs for 1,000 tough miles. I ran a good team. My leader was the bitch who birthed the other dogs."

The girls looked at each other.

"When Momma says something, the boys and girls do what she says," Mark explained. "My girl was a good dog."

Geoffrey was spread out beneath the table. He was so big that everyone, except Mary Rose, had tucked their feet under their chairs to make room for him. Mary Rose's feet, in real comfort, rested on Geoffrey's big rump.

When he heard, "dog" and "good dogs" Geoffrey opened one eye, perked up one ear, then went back to sleep.

Smart restaurant to let in good dogs.
He had done good work for them, too. He had eaten every single puff of spilled popcorn.

"Like you say," Mark Merrill continued, "Susan Butcher was a real champion. In one race, I was doing real good. I had on a red parka like this one." He nodded toward the coat hanging over the back of his chair. "And all at once a news helicopter started circling me. Well, I waved and thought how smart I was to wear red. I was going to be on tonight's news. I waved at the dudes in the chopper and they waved back and were filming like crazy."

"Then I hear, 'Trail! Trail!' behind me and Susan Butcher goes around me like I'm standing still." He grinned. "And the helicopter went right along with her."

They laughed, and Hadley wished that Mark lived at Meadow Lakes.

Wiley got up from the table, went to the bar, grabbed the two coffee pots and refilled regulars and decafs. Mark put so much sugar and cream in his coffee that Hadley laughed and accused him of making fudge.

"But another real champion, one with that Alaskan creative spirit, is John Suter," Mark went on. He was a good storyteller and obviously enjoyed this particular audience.

"Maybe it was because he was born in California," Mark said with a wink, "or maybe he's a descendant of Juan Quixote, but you gotta hear about The Poodle Man of the Iditarod."

They looked at each other. Marge shrugged. As usual, her red cane was hanging on the back of her chair.

"John Suter ran poodles." They looked at him in disbelief.

"Had a good team of twenty black, standard poodles, let their fur grow out, trained 'em by raising them with Huskies. See, Huskies have a little computer chip in their brains that says, 'Go! Run!' and Poodles have a chip that says, 'Lay back and be beautiful,' so Suter put the two breeds together and the Huskies taught the Poodles to run and be a team." He laughed. "Never worked the other way. Never saw a Huskie groomed with a tuft of fur on the end of its tail."

"How'd they do?" Wiley asked.

"Not bad! They finished every year and if you finish the Iditarod you're a winner. There are blizzards and trail hazards and sometimes 70 degrees below zero temperatures. One time, a big Swede racer went over to John and asked if he was really going to run Poodles and when John said, 'Yes', the Swede says, 'Yan, in Sveeden ve haf a saying. "Every village has its idiot." No different in Alaska.'" His accent made them all laugh.

"And one time, John was stopped in a village by a judge who thought he was running sheep because the Poodles' fur was so thick they looked like big black sheep." Mark took a long drink of coffee. "He was an inspiration, too. I remember getting up early one morning and hurrying because I wasn't going to let The Poodle Man beat me."

"Did he?" Robbie asked.

Mark just smiled.

They were quiet for a while.

Mary Rose went to the bathroom.

Robbie opened her computer and typed rapid notes.

When Mary Rose was back in her seat, Raven looked at Mark Merrill.

"Who's following us?" he asked.

They could tell Mark knew what Raven was talking about. He looked down at the table, shook his head, then nodded. When he looked back up at Raven, he said quietly, "Skinny little guy with expensive Muk-luks?"

Raven gave an almost imperceptible nod.

"That would be Boris Badenov."

"Oh, Sweet Jesus!" Robbie said. "That CANNOT be!"

They looked at her.

"Bullwinkle the Moose, Rocky the Flying Squirrel, and who was the villain in that children's television show?" She pointed at

Alphonso as if he had done something he shouldn't have, but it was Wiley who answered.

"The villain was Boris Badenov." It looked as if Wiley was ready to burst into laughter and fall off his chair.

Robbie dropped her head onto the table. When she raised it again, they were all laughing, even Mark Merrill who had no clue what was going on.

Raven's look told Mark to continue.

"He's harmless, at least as far as I know. He's hunted the jewels for years and always thought Betsy knew where they were. I don't know. He's scoured the dump for old furniture to take apart, and Betsy got all the good stuff, so that may be what's behind his thinking she has some. Of course," he smiled. "She does." They all remembered the old dog sled and the Calico Cat.

"Where do you think the jewels are, Mark?" Hadley asked.

"I don't really think there's a treasure trove from The Diamond Fund. If there is, it would be in the mines or caves. This was gold country, you know. There are treasures everywhere."

Mark looked at Raven and smiled. “I say Boris is harmless and I’ll stick with that feeling. I imagine if you catch up with the old rascal and just stand up next to him, he’ll back down and not bother you. As it is, he’s probably had more excitement following you than he’s had in years and like the Swede told John Suter,” he looked at them.

“Every village has an idiot and we’re entertaining yours,” Marge said, and she, without noticing what she was doing, reached behind herself and pulled her red cane onto her lap.

Part Five

The Blood-and-Thunder Trial of Buckshot Betsy Bushwhacker

From *The BOOB Girls, the Musical: BOOB Girl Song*

I think we overdid it. New bodies would be nice.
Perhaps a new approach,
and just for bravery girls,
How about applause?
You're saying "girls".
How about Burned Out Old Broads?
Burned Out Old Broads, you say?
Then claim it with pride!
Never live with regret. Live with nothing to hide.
Burned Out Old Broads - that's us!
The name is really perfect.
The acronym don't you see,
Burned Out Old Broads
B.O.O.B. Girls
Tell the world this is who we're gonna be!
Burned Out Old Broads
B.O.O.B. Girls
Tell the world this is who we're gonna be!
We claim it with pride!
Never live with regret. Live with nothing to hide.
This is who we're gonna be.
We wear it with pride.
BOOB Girls!

Opening Arguments

The first day of Betsy Bushwhacker's trial dawned bright and shining. Birds were singing and as they got out of the Hummer, Robbie pointed across the street where three Willow Ptarmigans, the state bird of Alaska, were feeding on birch seeds and berries that had snuggled into the grass. They were good-sized birds, and in their spring feathers, blended into the little park that apparently made a comfortable home for them.

"One of the few Arctic birds," Robbie told them. "They have feathers on their toes, so their feet won't freeze."

"What you need at night," Wiley said to Mary Rose, and he patted her on her fanny. She swatted his hand away and blushed.

The courthouse of Gospel Bird was a simple building, as was every building in the village. Cinder block, it had no ornate trim or any trim at all for that matter. It sat on a corner a block off of Gospel Bird's main street and housed everything from the DMV - Department of Motor Vehicles - to the local polling place. Animal control had a closet-sized office and officers kept themselves busy chasing foxes away from the local dump.

"It looks like a shrunken Walmart," Hadley observed as they approached the courthouse steps.

There was only one courtroom, and the friends were early, but not as early as Betsy, her attorney and the prosecutor. Raven had showered at the campground and left before any of the others were awake. He had taken Betsy to the Ill Eagle for breakfast and a briefing. She had caused a stir at the restaurant, with customers congratulating her on her shooting ability and wishing her good luck.

PickAxe Pete had not been overly popular, and he was certainly not going to win any beauty contests now.

The courtroom looked as if it had come from a different courthouse. The judge sat behind a huge hand-carved desk made of solid walnut. The witness stand was ornate walnut and looked frighteningly uncomfortable. Seats for the jury, behind what looked like a waist-high railing of burled walnut, looked only a little easier on the posterior.

Two tables with, of course, walnut chairs, faced the judge's bench. Separating them from the spectators was an attractive walnut barrier with a swinging gate that looked as if it were waiting for Perry Mason's private investigator, Paul Drake, to burst through with the evidence that would save the defendant and solve the murder.

They sat on the front row. Marge leaned her cane up against the barrier and they all settled in.

Betsy saw them and immediately hurried over. She leaned over the railing and hugged her cousin and greeted all the friends by name.

"Thank you again for bein' here for me," she smiled. "Mark said he had a good time with you all."

She looked good. Being a jailhouse bridge champion had served her well.

She looked at ease and confident.

So did Raven.

So did Slik Quick.

The only way to describe Slik was the word, "oily". He was tall, about six feet, with a sizeable paunch. It was one that made the decision about his pants difficult every morning. Should he start them above the paunch and let them slip down to barely hang over his hips, or start them there in the first place and spend rest of the day hitching them up? Either way, he would spend a lot of time messing with his pants.

His hair fit his name. It was slicked straight back and gave a new meaning to the old jar of butch wax. His suit had been expensive in the beginning, but now showed some wear and tear. It had been cleaned so many time the coat was a slightly different shade of brown than the pants. His brown shoes were polished and since he was sitting down, they could see one sock had lost its elasticity and slid down around his ankle.

"Needs support hose," Mary Rose whispered to Marge. Marge smiled and nodded.

Betsy had on a long yellow dress, brown boots and wore a cream-colored shawl around her shoulders. An attractive amethyst hung in the center of a gold chain around her neck.

Robbie pointed at Betsy and leaned toward Hadley. "One of the jewels?"

Hadley smiled and nodded.

Of the three people on the other side of the rail,

it was Raven who was attracting the attention of a rapidly growing crowd of spectators. He wore good-looking leather cowboy boots, jeans and a leather sports coat. His gold jewelry - a single chain, watch band and a Navajo ring, stood out against his brown skin. His greying braid hung below his shoulders.

"I thought he would lose the braid for the trial," Wiley whispered to Alphonso.

"Selling his Apache brand," Alphonso responded.

A bailiff, in uniform, entered the courtroom with the court reporter and they took their places near the bench. A huge regulator clock hung on one wall and at precisely nine o'clock, the door behind the bench opened and Judge Judge Jonkers arrived. He was short and balding with a jolly face that could make Santa Claus look grim. The judge looked like someone with whom you want to have lunch or a beer or at the very least, a long, heart-felt talk.

The bailiff bellowed out, "The Honorable Judge Judge Jonkers. All Rise!"

The crowd rose.

The judge stepped to his chair, which looked as expensive as Alphonso's over-priced office chair, swiveled it around so he could face the two tables, waved and nodded to several people in the crowd, and sat down.

"All right, Kiddies, what have we got here?"

"Betsy Bushwhacker and a charge of murder in the second degree, Your Honor," the bailiff said loudly enough for people passing by outside to know what was going on.

"I understand there will be no jury," Judge Jonkers said, glancing at Betsy. "You're going to leave the whole shebang up to me, that right counselors?"

"Yes, Your Honor," both attorneys said together. Betsy nodded vigorously.

Sheriff Malaprop arrived late and squirmed into a seat on the far-right side of the room. Judge Jonkers noticed him and scowled,

"I think I like the judge," Hadley whispered to Robbie. Both Robbie and Marge nodded in agreement. They had seen the look he had given Manley and the way he had smiled at Betsy.

"All right," the judge said, "who do we have here? Mr. Prosecutor, I know you well."

"Hello, Judge," Slik interrupted. Judge Jonkers looked mildly annoyed.

"Mr. Defense Attorney," the judge said, looking at Raven. "I have spoken with you by phone. It's nice to meet you. Your name is..."and he looked down at the papers before him.

"Raven, last name?"

"No last name, Your Honor."

"Your tribe is..."

"Apache, Your Honor."

"Apache," the judge looked carefully at the Indian who was smiling back at him.

"Apaches, according to my history, used to be the toughest, meanest Indians around."

Raven grinned and took a quick look at Slik Quick, then back at the judge. "What you mean used to be, white man?"

The judge laughed out loud. So did the crowd gathered in the visitors seats.

"Also admire that braid," the judge continued. "Natives in Alaska don't go in for that kind of stuff nor do attorneys who come before this court wear jeans with their braids."

"Trying to fit in, Your Honor."

The judge laughed again and Slik yelled, "Objection! You sound like you like him better than you do me, judge!"

"I do," the judge answered. "But then, nobody I know likes you, Slik."

More laughter from the gallery.

"Your Honor," Raven said. The two attorneys and Betsy were still standing. "I move to dismiss. Ms. Bushwhacker clearly did not intend to harm PickAxe Pete. It was an accident and there are no grounds for a murder charge."

The judge smiled. "I've read it, Counselor, and I tend to agree with you, but I hate to miss a good show. Let's get game on here."

The attorneys and Betsy sat.

Slik began his opening arguments. "Your Honor, the state will prove beyond a shadow of a doubt, that the accused intended, with malice aforethought, to maim, harm and kill her long-time lover, PickAxe Pete." He took a breath and the judge took advantage of it.

"Just for the record and my curiosity, what is PickAxe Pete's real name?" He looked at the audience.

The audience looked at each other. Raven looked at the judge. Betsy looked at the spectators and Slik looked annoyed. A few men met in the center aisle, talked for a minute, shrugged and sat back down.

"Okay, I think that answers that question," the judge said, and he nodded at Slik Quick to continue.

And Slik did. He not only continued, he went on and on and on! He gave Betsy's history, made up a history for PickAxe, managed to do a commercial for his law firm of one and all the time the clock ticked.

Hadley carefully pulled her tablet out and started to read her book.

Marge started polishing her red cane, particularly around the Taser jewel, and she noticed that Wiley and Mary Rose had a pad of paper between them and were into a hot game of tic-tac-toe.

Robbie slipped her computer onto her lap and was attempting to hide it with her purse and Hadley's purse.

Alphonso had his smart phone in his lap and had pushed his ESPN app.

Raven was in his zone and Betsy was staring straight ahead at nothing.

Maybe she had a zone, too.

The judge was fast asleep, as was at least one-third of the audience.

And still Slik kept on.

Once you're into something, never give up.

After a long hour, Slik banged his open hand on his table. Everyone woke up. Judge Jonker's chair tipped so far back Robbie gasped, sure he would topple over backward. He righted himself, tried to look dignified and settled his gaze on Slik.

"Thank you, Mr. Prosecutor. Mr. Raven for the defense?"

Raven stood. He was an impressive figure. There was total silence in the courtroom. Several people were leaning forward to make sure they heard every word.

"It was an accident."

Raven looked at the judge, put his hand on Betsy's shoulder and sat down.

There was a pause, then Judge Jonkers cleared his throat, moved some papers around in front of him and looked at Raven. "Appreciate your brevity, Mr. Raven!"

Raven smiled and nodded.

The judge looked at the clock on the wall. "It's a little early, but let's break for lunch. Let the court alert you, your judge is an old man with an old prostate." He looked out at the two attorneys and the audience. "A whole lot of you here are old men. You'll be pleased to know we'll be taking frequent prostate breaks in my courtroom."

As the judge stood up, he looked at the audience and spotted Alphonso.

"Hold it!"

Everyone stopped.

The judge squinted at Alphonso. "Alphonso..." he hesitated for a second, "Greatwood! The great wood himself. Kansas City Chiefs. Hell of a team when you were there. Can you get to my bench, Sir? I want to shake your hand."

"Oh. For Pete's sake!" Slik yelled. "Judge that's unfair to the prosecution."

"We're on break, Slik. And I don't have a clue what one of the greatest players in football history is doing in my courtroom, but I'm getting an autograph."

Alphonso got to his feet, grabbed his two canes and made his way toward the judge, who was about to find out what an old offensive lineman was doing in his courtroom.

Damn straight!

As she stood up and turned around, Marge caught a glimpse of the skinny man in Muk-luks sprinting out the big doors of the courtroom.

Witness, Witness

The courtroom was even more crowded after lunch. Slik Quick called his first witness.

"The state calls Dr. Benjamin Casey."

A tall, rotund gentleman in a flannel shirt and jeans took the witness stand and was sworn in.

"Dr. Casey," Slik began, "you are the medical examiner for this region, correct?"

"I am."

"And did you perform an autopsy on one PickAxe Pete?"

"I did."

"Before you performed the autopsy, did you check for a pulse?"

"No."

"Did you check for blood pressure?"

"No."

"Did you check for breathing?"

"No."

"So, then it is possible that the patient was alive when you began the autopsy?"

"No."

"How can you be so sure, Doctor?" Slik clasped his hands behind him and looked smug.

"Because his brain was sitting on my desk in a jar."

Doctor Casey looked up at the judge and shook his head. Judge Jonkers smiled and nodded. The entire courtroom snickered.

"Doctor, how many of your autopsies have you performed on dead people?"

"All of them. The live ones put up too much of a fight."

The spectators laughed out loud this time, and with all the dignity he processed, Slik Quick looked at Raven, said, "Your witness," and walked back to his chair.

Raven stood. "No questions, your Honor. I couldn't have done it better myself."

"Frankly, neither could I," the judge replied. "Doctor Casey, you are excused."

Slik stood again and called Digger O'Keefe, funeral director, to the stand. Digger waved at Betsy, nodded and smiled at the judge and was sworn in. He had over-dressed in a black suit and red, white and blue tie. He looked like a funeral director.

"Mr. O'Keefe, you buried one PickAxe Pete, correct?"

Slik sauntered over and leaned menacingly on the railing around the witness stand. To do this, he had to bend over a bit and his other sock rolled down to the top of his shoe.

"I did, and yes, he was very dead."

"Did you examine the body?"

"I did."

"And did you notice that PickAxe had been shot?"

"Hard to miss that one, half his head was gone."

"So. You would say he was definitely killed with a high-powered rifle,"

"I would."

Raven could have objected. PickAxe could have been killed by a high-powered rocket for that matter.

"And you are a qualified funeral director to judge the condition of the body, just as is the good Doctor Casey, correct?"

"Yep."

"Give us your qualifications, Mr. O'Keefe."

Digger looked a little puzzled then answered. "I did my apprenticeship at Burns and Ashe Crematorium in Ashville, South Carolina; I moved to Alaska and worked as an embalmer at the Italian funeral home, Amigone's in Fairbanks, then went on to Gross Funerals and Assman's in Anchorage. Been here at Dye and O'Keefe for ten years. Our motto is, 'Caskets so nice you'll want to die twice.'"

No one laughed this time. They all knew Digger's background. Robbie, however, sank lower in her pew-like seat with the mention of each name. Marge gripped her cane to keep from giggling and Wiley gripped Mary Rose's hand to make sure he didn't make a sound.

Slik spun around, looked at the crowd, then spun back toward Digger as he had seen done in old movies when the prosecutor was ready to deliver a fatal blow.

"Who paid for PickAxe Pete's funeral?" he asked loudly.

"Why. Betsy did. And she got a good price. She shoots 'em, we suit em." Digger laughed at his own joke and so did the crowd. As soon as the judge pounded the gavel, Digger went on, "If you're dead serious about saving money, check our prices."

Slik interrupted, "So, Betsy Bushwhacker paid for the funeral, after she had viciously murdered her lover, PickAxe Pete! No further questions." He swaggered to his seat.

"No questions, Your Honor," Raven said. He didn't bother to stand up.

Slik hadn't bothered to sit down. He hooked his thumbs into the pockets of the faded vest he wore, one that at one time matched his suit. Both thumbs appeared to get caught in the vest's lining. He tried working them free, gave up, left them captured by the lining and said, "Prosecution calls Sheriff Manley Malaprop."

Manley, in full uniform with gun at his side, swaggered better than Slik Quick to the stand and said, “I do!” as loudly as he could after the bailiff’s, “...so help me God.”

Slik, his thumbs still caught, wandered over to the witness stand.

“Sheriff, did you arrest one Betsy Bushwhacker for the murder of one PickAxe Pete?”

“I did.”

“When?”

The sheriff loyally gave the date, time and street address, which everyone in the courtroom knew was Digger O’Keefe’s funeral home driveway.

“And while this murderess was in your jail, did you hear her confess to murdering PickAxe Pete?”

“I did. She told my mother and her friends she had shot him in the head.” ‘Head’ came out as ‘haid,’ as Manley said it. Slik finally worked his thumbs out of his vest pockets and clasped them behind his back.

“Are you qualified to be Sheriff, Sheriff?”

Manley looked surprised and said, "I'm elected for Pete's sake, Slik."

"I see. So, while the prisoner was in your facility could she have escaped, and could you, with presence of mind and weapons on hand, accompanied her to the scene of the crime where you could have pursued the concept of multiple photographs, evidence collecting, and could you, having employed all the restraints of your office and using lessons from your training, could you have submitted to a full, written confession by said criminal?"

Manley's mouth fell open. "Slik, are you sure you passed the bar?"

The judge pounded the gavel. "Break time," he said, "Take ten. I have to pee."

Alphonso turned to Wiley. "That last question should be taken out and shot."

Wiley nodded. "If that was the rabbit Mark Merrill says Slik can pull out of a hat, it died a hard death on the way out".

"I think he asked that question in all one sentence without taking a breath," Robbie said.

Everyone stood up and stretched. Betsy leaned in toward Raven and they talked, the girls gathered in a little cluster, and Wiley and Alphonso followed the judge to find the men's room. Slik and Manley conferred, which included a lot of head-shaking by the Sheriff.

After the break, and as the judge took his seat, Alphonso leaned toward Marge. "You know how Manley asked Slik if he had passed the bar?" She nodded. "We were in the men's room with His Honor. The judge says after this he's going downtown and definitely not passing any bars." Marge snickered.

Slik turned Manley over to Raven, who walked slowly toward the witness stand, and not smiling at Manley asked, "Was Betsy a good prisoner?"

"She was awful! She tricked my crazy mother," he looked at the spectators, "and she IS crazy, into adopting her. Mama and her bridge friends decorated her cell, brought her books, played cards, taught her to crochet, and spoiled her with their home cooking! They made my jail smell, dammit, you know what happens when I bring in a new drunk or some other jailbird? They sniff and say it smells 'girly'. A jail should not smell girly. My jail smells like lavender!

Lavender, for Pete's sake."

With each statement, the Sheriff's voice became louder.

"She ruined my relationship with my Mama!"

Raven let the silence settle in around the sheriff, then he asked, "When you first saw PickAxe Pete's body, what did you do?"

"I arrested Betsy Bushwhacker for shooting his haid off!" The Sheriff was yelling.

"No, before that, sheriff, what did you do?"

Manley Malaprop took a long look at Raven, then he looked at the judge as if asking for help.

"You gotta answer, Manley, you're under oath," the judge said.

"I lost my cookies," Manley said softly. "I threw up."

"You threw up all over the undertaker's driveway. Understandable," Raven said softly, "No further questions Your Honor." He walked to his chair beside Betsy, the judge nodded at Manley and Manley bolted from the courtroom, his face bright red.

There was a rather long pause, then the judge looked at Slik. "Mr. Prosecutor, you got anyone else?"

Slik jumped a little, as if he hadn't expected the question, and said, "No, Your Honor, the prosecution rests."

"Mr. Raven?" the judge said.

Raven stood and said, "The defense calls Betsy Bushwhacker."

Betsy's Testimony

Betsy walked to the witness stand. She was almost as tall as Raven and she looked fresh and rested as she put her hand on the Bible and took the oath.

"Ms. Bushwhacker, did you kill PickAxe Pete?"

"I did. But I didn't mean to. See, he had on these high-heeled boots and had lifts in them, and that made him taller than usual, and when I aimed over his head, I hit his head."

"You're a good shot."

"The best, Raven. I can hit a tin can from so far away I almost can't see it."

"Your Honor," Raven said, walking toward the bench, "I'd like to present a short demonstration."

The judge nodded for him to go ahead.

He walked to the defense table, bent over and pulled out a rifle. He held it up, so everyone could see it.

"This is loaded," he said, looking around, "and

the court will notice a target on the far wall."
He pointed to the figure of a man taped to the courtroom wall on the judge's far left. It was the kind of figure used in shooting galleries and for law enforcement target practice.

"I would like Ms. Bushwhacker to show us how accurately she can shoot."

"Good!" the judge said. "I was hoping for some action."

Raven walked toward the witness stand, handed Betsy the rifle and motioned for her to step down and to stand as far across the room as possible. She climbed into the jury box, took a position behind the last row of chairs, took quick aim and fired one shot. It hit the target square and directly between the legs.

There was a communal gasp from the audience.

She took aim again, fired once more, and got a hit directly into the target's heart.

Her third and last shot took off the target's head.

The crowd applauded, the judge smiled and tapped his gavel, and Raven collected the gun.

"She could have faced the wall behind her, held the gun over her shoulder, turned her head and done it again," Marge whispered to Alphonso. He agreed.

Betsy sat back down, Raven stood over her, smiled and said, "It was an accident."

Betsy nodded vigorously and said softly, "Yes."

Raven turned her over to Slik, who did another swagger toward the witness stand and glared at Betsy.

"Buckshot Betsy Bushwhacker, when is your birthday?"

"June 23."

"What year?"

"Every year."

Judge Jonkers dropped his head to his big desk. You could see his shoulders moving up and down as he laughed without making a sound.

"And were you married to PickAxe Pete?"

"No! We were in a romantic relationship. If we

had been married, we would NOT have been in a romantic relationship! You know that, Slik, you were married once."
"But you have been married?"

"Yes"

"And how was your marriage terminated?"

"By death."

"Whose death was it?"

Betsy looked at the judge. "Judge, can I have a different prosecutor?"

Judge Jonkers shook his head. "Sorry dear, we're all stuck with him. Go on, Slik?"

"You murdered PickAxe Pete!" Slik twirled around toward the spectators when he said it, then back toward Betsy. "You have already confessed."

"I killed him, but it was an accident."

"Had you ever killed him before?"

Betsy looked at the judge again. The judge shrugged.

"No, when I kill someone, I only do it once and they stay dead."

"Were you alone or by yourself when you pulled the trigger."

"If somebody else was there, I'd be blamin' them!"

Slik put his hands behind his back and walked in a small circle for a minute.

"Ms. Bushwhacker, have you lived in Gospel Bird all your life?"

Betsy smiled. "Not yet, Slik."

"When you shot PickAxe, where did you aim?"

"Above his head."

"And where was his head?"

"Just above his shoulders."

Alphonso leaned toward Marge. "A major network should be filming this."

The questioning went on for another forty-five minutes, firmly establishing that Betsy was definitely in the courtroom and that Slik should have gone into his father's roofing company.

When Slik was done, the judge announced another potty break, promised he would drink no more coffee and when he returned to the bench, looked at the clock and said they would hear closing arguments if the prosecution could keep his statements to half an hour.

Slik took thirty-eight minutes, spoke to the spectators as well as the Judge, and sat down with a satisfied smile on his homely face.

The judge looked at Raven. "Mr. Defense Attorney. Closing arguments."

Raven stood up, looked at Slik, then spoke to the judge. "It was an accident."

He sat down.

The judge took a deep breath, leaned his arms on his desk and surveyed the audience. He glanced at Betsy, then Raven, then Slik. "Often in courtrooms where the judgment is up to the judge, we of the judiciary will announce a time in the near future when we will deliver a verdict. However, in this case, the results are clear. Will the defendant and attorneys please rise?"

Slik, Raven and Betsy stood up. The girls held their breath.

"I find Ms. Bushwhacker not guilty of the murder of PickAxe Pete of no last name. I agree with the defense, it was an accident and I swear never to wear high-heeled boots with lifts in 'em."

Raven hugged Betsy, Slik looked defeated. The girls hugged. Alphonso slapped Wiley on the back and the judge pounded his gavel.

All was quiet in the courtroom.

"I brought my fishing equipment," the judge announced. "Slik, you have everything you need to do some fly fishing, and you have enough waders for Mr. Greatwood and his friend. Mr. Raven would you join us tomorrow for some excellent fishing on the Gospel Bird River?"

Raven nodded and so did Alphonso and Wiley.

What a guy thing.

As they started to leave their seats and move into the crowded aisle of the courtroom, Mary Rose McGill stopped suddenly. "Wait!" she said. She turned, pushed Wiley out of the way and scurried through the railing to the judge's desk, where he was packing up the papers from the trial.

The judge looked at her with curiosity. "Yes, my dear?"

"Judge," Mary Rose said, a little out of breath, "do you know where I can find an Inukshuk?

Fishing for Jewels

"So, what do we want to do while the boys throw funny-looking lines in the water?" Robbie asked. They were sitting around the table in the trailer, Geoffrey lay at their feet snoring his soft doggie snore. Marge had a smile from ear to ear.

"We've been in all the little shops in Gospel Bird," Hadley said.

"Betsy and her new friends are playing bridge in her cabin while Mark Merrill replaces her door. They aren't available to do anything," Robbie observed.

There was a moment of silence and they all looked at the grinning Marge, who was quietly turning her cane over and over on her lap.

"What?" Hadley asked,

"Marge Aaron, what are you thinking with that stupid grin?" Robbie asked.

Mary Rose reached her foot out, rubbed Geoffrey and looked questionably at her large, grinning friend,

Marge leaned her cane against the table, then

leaned in herself. She looked for a second at each BOOB girl. "We're going to follow the treasure map into the cave or mine, whichever it is."

"Oh, my gosh," Mary Rose said. "I'd forgotten all about the jewels and the little map."

Hadley got up from the table, walked a few feet and retrieved her purse. She dug into it and found the little drawstring bag where she kept the map. Taking it out and laying it on the table, she smiled at Marge. "Detective Aaron, you are one party animal!"

Marge smoothed the piece of paper that contained the crude drawing and they all leaned in to take a look. "We'll have to slip around Betsy's cabin, because of her bridge game and Mark's carpentry, but it looks as if the road in front of the cabin keeps going until we get to..." she leaned in closer to the map.

"Robbie can you tell what that is?"

Robbie leaned in as well. "It looks like a sign, but I can't see what's on it."

"Okay," Marge leaned back in her chair, put her hands down flat on the table and looked at them. "We tell the boys we're going shopping. This is ours and ours alone."

Mary Rose stood up and held out her hand, palm facing them. "B.O.O.B. Girls! Wear it with pride!" They all stood, put their hands together and said, "BOOB Girls! Burned Out Old Broads!"

Wiley Vondra was doing his best to convince Mary Rose. "He would have so much fun, honey, and I could keep him from splashing around and scaring the fish. The judge and Slik know a place where Alphonso can get to on his scooter and we can tie him to the bitch seat and he'll be good and then he can run around all he wants when we're done fishing."

All the girls wanted the protection and nose of the big mastiff when they were in the cave or mine.

"No, Wiley, he'd be a real distraction and what's more we want...we want..."

"To groom him," Hadley yelled from the door of the trailer. "Just smell that dog, Wiley Vondra. He stinks to high heaven."

Wiley Vondra had no sense of smell.
"He can bounce around in the water, Hadley."

Wiley yelled back.

"The judge won't like that, and are you willing to take two towels and the doggie shampoo with you and bathe him in the river?"

"Sounds like a baptism," Marge said to Robbie. They were in the trailer, watching Mary Rose and Wiley yell back and forth at Hadley and argue outside.

Geoffrey was doing an Olympic-class 'sit' beside Mary Rose, his head going back and forth between her and Wiley. He cocked an ear when Hadley yelled.

"Crap!" was all Wiley said.

"Whew," was all Robbie and Marge said together.

Wiley gave Mary Rose a quick kiss. As he turned away, she turned toward Hadley and gave the faces peering out from door and window a quick two thumbs up.

In about half an hour, Alphonso's van pulled out of the RV park. Five minutes later, the Hummer left behind it.

They were quiet on the road to Betsy's cabin.

Hadley took a CD out of its box and slipped it into the Hummer's player. In seconds a deep, resonate voice began reading Robert Service poems. They listened, entranced.

Geoffrey was in his space in the back of the Hummer, looking out to see where he had been.

As soon as they spotted Betsy's cabin ahead of them, Marge pulled the Hummer to one side of the rut-infested, rough road and turned it off. It leaned into the ditch and Hadley took ahold of the sissy bar above her head. They watched and listened. There was an older Dodge parked in front of the cabin, and since Mark Merrill drove a truck, they assumed the Dodge had brought the bridge players. A trail of smoke drifted out of the chimney and there was no movement to be seen.

"Looks like Mark's done with the door," Marge said. "He doesn't seem to be around."

Marge started the big vehicle and they slowly and steadily rolled past the cabin. It wasn't until they were well past it that they realized they had all been holding their breaths. They let out a communal breath together and laughed.

"Onward and upward!" Marge said, as the

Hummer dug in and began to climb the trail up the mountain.

Marge stopped to let a brown bear cross the path. Later on, Robbie pointed to three beautiful deer watching them from the brush on the passenger side. Squirrels jumped from tree to tree across the road and a flock of wild turkeys made the Hummer stop again, this time for five or six minutes.

Caught in the Depths of the Mine

They drove on...and on...and on. The road became narrower still, and in almost every minute tree branches or straggly bushes brushed against the Hummer. They bounced. Geoffrey yipped now and then when Marge hit one of the larger holes or ran over a boulder.

"Good thing we have a Hummer," Marge mumbled as she gripped the steering wheel so tightly her knuckles turned white.

At one point, they forded a fast-running little stream that came halfway up to their fenders. Hadley held her breath, Robbie crossed her fingers, Marge mumbled louder, and Mary Rose prayed. Geoffrey tried to stand up and immediately fell over on his side. He yipped again.

They spoke very little. They were all hanging on. After nearly an hour, Mary Rose was obviously uncomfortable. Hadley was first to notice that her friend had a grimace on her face and that her grip on the back of the seat behind Marge was making her knuckles as white as the driver's.

"Mary Rose, what's going on, honey?" she asked.

"I really, really have to pee," Mary Rose said, a whine in her voice, "and Geoffrey does, too. I can always tell. His eyes cross and his tongue hangs out. I think my eyes and tongue are doing the same thing."

"Stick with it for a minute," Marge said. "I'll watch for a wide spot in the road."

"Why?" Robbie asked. "We haven't seen another car since we got on this crazy trail."

"Good point," Marge said, and in just minutes she had found what could only be described as the widest spot in the road; one that was almost non-existent.

She stopped the Hummer and turned it off. They all climbed out.

"I'm going to join her," Robbie announced,

Marty Rose fastened Geoffrey's leash to his collar and hurried into the woods, Robbie right behind her. Geoffrey found a tree in the first ten seconds out of the car.

"Watch out for wood rats!" Marge yelled after them.

"Thanks, girlfriend," Robbie yelled back, "watching for rats is one of our favorite hobbies."

Hadley and Marge stretched and walked down the trail for about a minute. Marge used her cane for every step. "It's truly beautiful," Hadley said, looking around at the forest-covered mountain. In the distance, they could hear a waterfall rumbling down a mountainside. The air was filled with birdsong and it was immensely peaceful and quiet.

Until Mary Rose McGill began to yell.

"Hadley! Marge! Come here! Come here, quick!"

They turned and hurried toward Mary Rose's voice. "Where are you?" Hadley yelled back. All she and Marge could see were trees and dense brush.

"Little path about six steps from the Hummer!" Robbie yelled.

They saw the footprints and followed them a few yards.

"I hope she hasn't peed on another foot," Hadley said, more to herself than to Marge. Once again,

Hadley remembered how, in the first year the girls had been together, Mary Rose had scurried into the woods and ended up peeing on a dead man's foot.

In another minute, they were standing beside Robbie and Mary Rose, who were breaking branches away from in front of a large sign. They moved in and all four of them tore and pulled at branches, bushes and vines. Geoffrey, whose leash had been dropped on the ground, jumped around and barked. "Play!" he loved "play!"

"What does it say?" Hadley asked. They stood in front of an old, dilapidated wooden sign that had once stood tall and proud.

T-E UNLU–Y S–IKE MI-E

That was all they could make out. Some of the letters were entirely missing or wiped out.

Robbie got it right away. "THE UNLUCKY STRIKE MINE"

"Right!" Hadley and Mary Rose said together. Marge pulled out the map. They gathered around her and looked at it.

"It could be," Marge said, "It could be."

Geoffrey was digging in an open space of dirt. "What are you finding, Geoff?" Mary Rose asked.

"Something dog-like," Robbie said, "but look."

She pointed past the big mastiff to what looked like the edge of an opening in the mountain. "That's the mine entrance I betcha."

They pushed branches from bushes aside as they made their way slowly toward where Robbie pointed. When they reached it, and pulled more branches and even some small bushes aside, they could see what was left of an old mine entrance. A large, dark, foreboding hole loomed before them. "Yep," Robbie said, "we found it." She shivered just a little.

"Stay here, don't move," Marge said. As quick as she could limp and hobble, she hurried back to the Hummer, Geoffrey circling her and bouncing along happy as a dog in the woods

They waited.

"What's she doing?" Mary Rose asked. Hadley and Robbie both shrugged. In just a few minutes, Marge hurried back, breathing a little heavily, Geoffrey loyally beside her.

"In case our cell phone flashlights lose their batteries," Marge breathed, and handed Hadley a large flashlight.

"We had one in the Hummer and I sneaked into the van and got this bigger one from Alphonso's tool box."

"Marge Aaron, you were planning this all along," Robbie said. "That's why you asked us last night if our cell phones were charged and made sure they were all hooked up."

"Marge Aaron, homicide detective, retired," Marge grinned. "Let's go." And she led the way into the total darkness of the mine.

"Holy Moly," Robbie said, and she followed Marge into the darkness.

"God help us," Hadley said.

"Jesus, Mary and Joseph," Mary Rose said.

"Move it girls, we haven't got all day," Marge said.

Geoffrey, with his doggie eyes, had already bounced ahead of them into the abyss. They walked carefully, each with one hand against the wall of the tunnel.

“What are we looking for?” Robbie asked.

“A box? A pipe, anything that could hold jewels, I guess.” Hadley said.

“No dead bodies, though,” Mary Rose said. “I’m swearing off finding dead bodies.”

“Hellloooo!!” Robbie yelled, trying for a good echo.

“Hellooo” came back to them.

“Geoffreeey!” Mary Rose yelled. She was starting to get worried about her dog, He could be anywhere in this cavernous and creepy place. “Geofreeey!” echoed back at her.

“Where are you, Geoff? Where are you, Romanov treasure?” Robbie yelled again, cupping one hand to her mouth.”

“Right behind you!” came the voice, but it wasn’t an echo.

They stopped short and turned. Standing in his Muk-luks and pointing a big gun at Marge ‘s face was Boris Badenov.

“Oh, Dear,” Mary Rose said.

“Oh shit.” Marge said, looking at the gun.

Together, Hadley and Robbie said, “Geoffrey!”

Geoffrey did not appear.

“I was just about ready to turn around and go back,” Badenov said, an evil grin spreading over his ugly face. “Not easy following you along Shingletown Ridge. Hell of a road. Gotta give it to you for driving it, lady.” All the time he was talking he looked at Marge, who was holding her cane and unable to do a thing with it.

“You mean you haven’t already looked for the jewels here in the mine?” Hadley asked.

“Not logical,” Robbie said. She did a good job of impersonating Star Trek’s Mr. Spock.

“Oh, I’ve looked here, and the jewels are here, all right. Some priceless necklaces, a tiara, diamonds, you name it. Found them last year, but I always came in at the main entrance, boarded up, but I made a space in it big enough to crawl through. You found the back entrance, closed when the mine went out twenty years ago.”

“So. Why leave them here?” Marge asked.

"Oh, I didn't leave them all," Boris grinned. "I put them back where I found them and just took a few out at a time. Took 'em to San Francisco where I have a partner who fences them for a good price. Too many at once gets suspicious." His chest puffed out a little. He liked bragging about how smart he had been.

"Where were they hidden, Boris?" Marge asked. If she had been interrogating a homicide suspect, she would have a six-pack of beer, cigarettes and chips to lure him into telling her secrets. Unfortunately, none of that was available, but her soothing voice seemed to be getting the job done.

"Way down a shaft close to this one. Turns a corner and heads west. They were buried in a hole in the wall and covered with a pile of rocks. I was picking the rocks up, thinking there might be some gold there and ta dah. There they were."

"Very clever," Hadley said.

"Lucky strike in the Unlucky Strike," Robbie said, remembering the name of the mine."

"I have to pee again," Mary Rose said.

"And what about us?" Marge asked.

"When you gotta go, you gotta go. And you gotta go," Boris answered.

"Thank goodness," Mary Rose said. "I'd hate to pee here in the dark."

"No, lady, I mean I'm going to kill you."

"Oh."

"But we have to wait awhile until the man you brought comes back to see what's happened to his lady friends." Boris chuckled. "He that other dude in the brown leather vest who was with you at the trial?"

The girls looked at each other. Then they realized Boris thought Geoffrey was a man, not a dog.

"I still have to pee," Mary Rose said. She moved a step closer to Boris Badenov. "I'm going to walk down the tunnel a little way, I'll take a flashlight, and keep it on so you can see where I am." She stared into his eyes. "But I am going to pee!" she reached out and grabbed Marge's flashlight. Hadley's light was focused on Boris's gun, and all their cell phone flashlights were on, making the area around them very visible.

"Uh, okay," Boris managed to say. Then he gave her a mean look, moved the gun from its aim at Marge and grabbed Robbie around the neck. He held her against his chest, his arm firmly around her, gun pointed at her head. "One misstep and your friend here is dead. No one ever comes into this part of the mine. No one will find your bodies."

"Deal," Mary Rose said, "I'll be right back," and with the light shining in front of her, she started down the steep incline of the tunnel.

They were all quiet.

"What's she doing?" Boris asked.

"If you have to ask, you're not as smart as you think you are," Hadley said.

"She's saying something," Boris said loudly, then even louder he asked, "What's she saying?"

"She always talks to herself when she goes to the bathroom," Marge said, as if he were a kindergartner who didn't get it.

"Hurry up, lady!" he yelled.

The girls could make out what Mary Rose was

saying. It was, "Geoffrey, treat, here Geoffrey, treat." It wasn't loud, but it was good enough for doggie ears. "Play!" Mary Rose yelled as the big mastiff bounced up the tunnel floor, his tongue hanging out, his strong legs pumping. "Play!' Mary Rose yelled again, and she pointed at Boris.

Robbie stomped on Boris's foot with all her might.

"Ow! That hurt!" Boris screamed. The surprise made him let go of his grip around her neck.

As Geoffrey flew through the air to take Boris down, Marge pushed her cane's smoke screen jewel. They heard Boris hit the ground with a thud as the big dog landed on him. Geoffrey barked a playful bark and bounced out of the smoke that filled the tunnel. He hurried over beside Marge.

He knew where the action was coming from.

Boris was getting up as the smoke cleared. And Marge pushed the button for tripping pellets. The pellets crashed down onto the tunnel floor and Boris began what looked like a weird, uncoordinated dance seen only at wedding receptions. "What the...!" he yelled

Geoffrey joined him in the dance, then quickly decided it was a people play thing, not good for dogs. Boris cleared a space in the pebbles with his boots and bent to get his gun. That's when Marge Aaron tasered him in the balls. He went down with an even louder thud.

Marge pushed the jewel on her cane that sends knives out the sides. She took one knife, opened the tip of the cane and pulled out the gold lariat inside. "Tie him up," she told the girls, cutting off a long section of lariat. "I have one more thing to do." She went back up the tunnel to the mine entrance, took a step outside, and pushed the jewel on the cane that turned it into a rifle.

The girls heard the shot.

"What's she shooting at?" Mary Rose asked as she tied up Boris. Hadley held her finger in the knot like you do when putting ribbon on Christmas packages.

Marge came back in just seconds. "I never get to use all the stuff on this cane in one day," she explained.

Goodbye Sourdoughs

Marge studied the knots Mary Rose had tied in the rope around Boris' wrists and ankles.

"Where did you learn knots like that, girlfriend?"

"I'm a mother. I had Brownie Troops and Girl Scout Troops," Mary Rose said proudly.

Boris was laying on his stomach, swearing a blue streak.

"I thought about hog-tying him," Mary Rose said, her hands on her hips, "but if his wrists and ankles were tied together, we'd have to drag him to the Hummer and frankly, Marge, we're just getting too old for that." She was nodding in agreement with herself as she spoke.

"I think it's a beautiful tie-up," Hadley said.

"Mary Rose has talents we've never discovered," Robbie agreed.

Boris was the one who did an eye roll this time, and just kept on swearing.

"Frankly, Mr. Badenov," Mary Rose said, her

hands still on her hips, "I really am offended at your language. Now shut the hell up!"

The other three looked at each other and grinned.

Boris shut the hell up.

They all worked together to pull him to his feet. He wasn't moving. He started to swear again, and Mary Rose simply said, "Geoffrey, play!"

It is not comfortable being hit in the back by a flying, oversized mastiff. Even when lying down. Geoffrey put his nose under Boris' ribs and rolled him over on his back, where he began to lick his face with vigor and obvious satisfaction.

"Ow! Quit it!" Boris yelled.

Geoffrey kept lapping away, doggie droll running down the old miner's cheek.

"Boris," Hadley said in a kindly voice, "we can keep doing this all day. We only have to take breaks for Mary Rose to pee, but we'd really like to get back before dark. None of us likes driving after dark and our three men, along with the judge and Slik..." she looked at Robbie, "did Manley go with them?"

"Nope, you got them all."

"They'll be looking for us, and you really don't want Alphonso, Wiley and especially Raven pissed at you."

"And believe me," Marge added, "they will be."

"Okay, okay, you win for now you..." Boris looked at Mary Rose and put the brakes on his next word. "Help me up, dam...I mean dang it."

It took all four of them to pull, push and lift Boris upright again. He began to hop toward the tunnel entrance and they followed him, slowly. He kept hopping as they headed for the Hummer.

"Actually, that's about the speed I like to walk," Robbie told Hadley as they made their way slowly up the brush-covered trail. Mary Rose led the strange procession, frequently holding branches out of the way.

No one said much.

"Those are great Muk-luks," Robbie said to Boris, "where did you get them?"

"Hudson Bay company, but they're the real

McCoy. Made by Eskimos."

"Nice." Hadley added.

BOOB Girls. Fashion experts even in a crisis.

"All right," Marge said when they got to the Hummer. She lifted the back gate and Geoffrey jumped in. "Here's your seat, Boris. Put your butt on the floor of that back gate, swing your legs around and lay down."

"With that dumb dog?" Boris said loudly.

"Shhhh," Mary Rose said, putting her finger over her mouth, "or I'll say the 'P' word."

Boris looked puzzled.

"P-l-a-y," Mary Rose spelled it out.
Both Boris and Geoffrey looked at her. She nodded.

Boris sat down close to the big dog, and Hadley grabbed his ankles and lifted his legs into the back compartment. He took one look at Geoffrey and didn't fight it.

Geoffrey looked at him with the same grin he had when Mary Rose cut up pieces of meat for him.

They got in the Hummer, and Marge backed up to the still-narrow wide spot in the road. She spent a good ten minutes maneuvering the big vehicle back and forth until she got it turned around and headed down the trail toward Gospel Bird.

"Good job, Marge!" Robbie said.

"Expert at the wheel," Hadley said.

"You are the best," Mary Rose finished.

"This dumb dog is licking me again!" Boris said.

"Smnuff," Geoffrey said.

Happy travelers, on their way to town.

The road was just as bad going down the other way, but as always happens, it seemed to go faster coming back than going out. There were no cars at all parked at Betsy's cabin when they rolled by and got onto a better stretch of the road. Her pickup was missing, too.

"Bet she's in town," Marge said.

Geoffrey and Boris were quiet.

"What are we going to do with our friend in the back?" Hadley asked.

"How about we drop him off with Manley, tell the sheriff where the jewels are and let him feel good about himself for a change." Marge suggested.

"He threatened to kill us," Mary Rose said. "Are we pressing charges?"

"I wasn't going to kill you!" Boris yelled.

His yelling made Geoffrey lick his face again.

"I know," Marge said. "I could see into the chamber of that old gun he held in my face. It wasn't loaded."

"Where is his gun?" Robbie said, looking around as if she could find it on the seat beside her.

"In my pocket," Marge said. "And I was right. It's not loaded."

They rode in silence for a while.

"What if Manley throws up when we deliver Boris?" Mary Rose asked.

"He won't," Marge said, "Boris has a lot of his head left."

Mary Rose thought of something and turned toward the back, "Boris, since you know where to get things, where can I find an inukshuk?"

Sheriff Manley Malaprop looked at Boris Badenov and his mouth hung open.

"What the heck are you women doing?" he asked, looking at Marge, who was quietly pointing her cane at the still-tied-up Boris. Geoffrey was doing his Olympic-class sit at her feet. A good back up dog.

"Delivering a prisoner, Sheriff," Marge said.

"We saw what kind of man you are when you let your mother adopt Betsy when she was in jail," Hadley said with a smile.

"You're the kind of sheriff every town needs," Robbie added.

"And now you can be a hero in Gospel Bird," Mary Rose said.

"Crap," Boris said.

Geoffrey growled, Marge lifted her cane and Boris shut up.

“What did he do?” Manley asked, “try to make out with one of you? I know Boris and he can be that stupid all right.”

“He stole from the town,” Marge said.

“He threatened to kill us with an empty gun,” Mary Rose added.

“His lack of intelligence is exceeded only by his stupidity,” Robbie said.

“And he is a general nuisance and poor dresser,” Hadley said. “With the exception of his Mukluks.”

Manley smiled. “I think I’ll stick with the ‘stole from the town’ accusation.”

“He’s found some of the Romanov jewels in the old Unlucky Strike Mine,” Marge told him. “I know enough law to know that when the mine closed, the property reverted back to Gospel Bird. He’s been taking the jewels to San Francisco and fencing them.” She pointed her cane at Boris. “That is stealing from the town.”

“I wondered how he could afford those Muk-luks," Manley said, shaking his head.

"They come from the Hudson Bay Company, but they were made by Eskimos," Mary Rose informed him.

"He threatened you, and you took him down?" Manley said, still shaking his head.

"We did," the girls said together.

"Never underestimate a burned out old broad," Robbie said.

"B.O.O.B Girls!" they said together.

Manley shook his head one more time.

"Leave him here, ladies," Manley said, as if they planned to keep Boris for a pet. "Boris Badenov, you are under arrest for grand theft."

Now it was Boris' turn to shake his head. "Listen, Manley," he started to say. Geoffrey growled deep in his throat and Boris shut up again.

"This is just like in those Cozy Mystery books," Mary Rose said as they went out the door. "The villain ends up in jail and the women win."

"Just like the University of Nebraska Women's Volleyball Team," Hadley said.

"Go Big Red," Robbie and Marge said together.

They found the boys having a pitcher of beer at the Ill Eagle. Waitress was putting a gigantic plate of nachos in the center of their table.

"How was fishing?" Mary Rose asked, pulling up a chair next to Wiley and patting him on the shoulder. They gathered around the table and dug into the nachos. The judge and Slik had left after one beer and now the seven friends were back together and back to normal.

Robbie was sitting by Raven, her hand once again on his knee. Marge and Alphonso were side-by-side and Geoffrey, a loving, sensitive dog, curled up at Hadley's feet.

"Fishing was pretty good," Alphonso said, "I could get to the bank of the river in the Green Machine, and the only disgusting part was my buddy here." He pointed at Raven.

"What did he do?" Robbie asked.

"He catches the fish with his hands!" Alphonso answered. "Stripped off his shirt and boots, waded into the water and caught fish with his bare hands. Show off!"
"Apache Indian trick," Raven said.

"Well," Marge said, "we did have a bit of an

adventure. You know that little map we found that was supposed to lead to the Romanov jewels..." and together the girls filled them in on Boris, the mine, and the jewels.

After they finished, there was total silence.

"That is just fantastic," Waitress said. She had been standing close to them, listening carefully.

"We cannot only not take you out in public," Alphonso said with a smile, "we can't trust you when you go out alone."

"As Robbie told Manley," Hadley said, "never underestimate a burned out old broad."

"You want to go home?" Wiley said, looking at the girls, "Omaha sounds pretty good to me right now."

Raven squeezed Robbie's hand. "I leave tomorrow. The guys thought they could drop me off in Anchorage, then head down the Cassair Highway toward Washington state."

Robbie nodded, her eyes a little teary.

"Somebody else mentioned the Cassair," Mary Rose said, trying to remember.

"Short term memory goes first," Wiley told her.

On the Road Again

It would be a five-day trip, maybe six. They all felt immensely lucky. No one had gotten sick or hurt. No one had even fallen and not been able to get up. Betsy had given them long, tearful hugs when they said goodbye. Manley had wished them well. Slik had waved at them from the window of his one-man law office, and the judge had called Alphonso and passed on his good wishes.

"I guess my only regret is that I didn't find my Inukshuk," Mary Rose said as they left Anchorage after taking Raven to the airport.

"Order it online, girlfriend," Robbie told her.

"Not the same," Mary Rose replied.

Robbie had directed them to the Ulu factory in Anchorage, and they had all purchased the beautiful Eskimo knives that were invented hundreds of years ago. They were one of the most interesting, versatile and attractive cutting instruments ever created. The girls had gotten them for themselves and for gifts. Each Ulu had its own, specially carved cutting board.

The Cassair Highway meets the Alcan near Watson Lake. They stayed an extra day in the campground there to rest and shop. Everyone had a relative or friend to whom they wanted to give a gift from Alaska or someplace along the Alcan, and the Ulus would be saved for special gifting.

In every shop, Mary Rose asked about an Inukshuk. “It’s a beautiful figure made of stones that Eskimos put together to mark where they have found game,” she explained each time. She became the Inukshuk teacher of half of Canada and Alaska it seemed.

Jade City

It was their second day on the Cassair when Robbie, looking at the Milepost Magazine, found a place to stop for lunch.

"Jade City," she said from her back seat in the Hummer. It's not a town, but it has a huge jade mine and is a little settlement with what is described as one of the best gift shops along either the Alcan or Cassair highway.

Mary Rose frowned. "Somebody mentioned Jade City, but I don't remember who or why."

"Who doesn't like jade?" Hadley asked.

Cellphone service was active, so Mary Rose called Wiley and told him they had a lunch stop spotted ahead at Jade City.

The sun was bright as they pulled into the big parking lot at the place where the huge sign welcomed tourists and their money to Jade City. There were behemoth trucks filled with gigantic rocks that must have been jade-in-the-rough. A big log cabin contained both restaurant and gift shop.

Mary Rose and Wiley both headed for the little building that contained restrooms. Alphonso rolled out of the van and steered his two canes up the wooden sidewalk toward the restaurant. Hadley, Marge and Robbie went inside, then Robbie dashed out as fast as she could.

"Mary Rose," she yelled, "Mary Rose McGill, hurry up!" She dashed into the ladies' room still yelling, "Hurry!"

Mary Rose hurried. Robbie almost pushed her into the gift shop.

There, on two walls lined with wooden shelves, were hundreds of Inukshuks. They were in all sizes and made from jade and rock and limestone. They were beautiful. There was one at $5,000 and many for $500 and even more for $100, small but perfect.

Mary Rose picked out a small white one, held it to her chest and said, "I just love this!" Wiley made a purchase right after Mary Rose checked out, and Alphonso picked up a new wallet. Robbie, Hadley and Marge came out with jade earrings.

The hamburgers weren't half bad, either.

Epilogue

Summer had slipped in unannounced when they returned to Meadow Lakes Retirement Community. The trees were in full, brilliant leaf, the flowering borders around the big apartment building were blooming their hearts out, with early roses filling the air with a gentle, rich scent. The lawns were a luxuriously green and perfectly groomed.

They dropped the trailer off in the storage area where it spent most of its time.

"It's really dirty," Mary Rose said.

Both the Hummer and Alphonso's van were encrusted with dust and grime from the 1300 miles of Alcan Highway. They had driven in a couple of rainstorms coming home, and the rain had not acted to rinse the vehicles off. Instead, it had acted as a strong glue that kept everything clinging to the sides, roofs and hoods. The dusty windshields had ugly clean areas where they had been washed by turning on the windshield washers.

They were too tired to wash them.

But they were home.

"I can't wait for a movie marathon!" Mary Rose said, joyously. "We can do movies filmed in Alaska, like 'Insomnia,' with popcorn with M&Ms and goldfish crackers."

Sheryl had done a masterful job of keeping things in order. Alphonso had checked in with her every chance he got and whenever he had cell service.

Two residents had died while they had been gone.

"When you're as old as we are," Robbie observed, "you go to more and more funerals."

Once again, they were grateful they had survived their adventure in good health and proud that they had made the trip.

One couple they knew at Meadow Lakes had moved to an assisted living complex, and Hadley put words to how lucky they were.

"Ever this day, I resolve - to find bits of happiness, to laugh, to recognize joy and beauty and to live a life of gratitude, for I am a lucky, happy woman."

They all showered, put on super casual clothes and took a nap. As Marge had pointed out, naps weren't just a privilege anymore. They were a necessity.

They ate dinner in Meadow Lakes big dining room and were the center of attention.

Alphonso looked around the dining room. "As we said when we left, half the people here envy us, and the other half are relived it wasn't them."

After dinner, Hadley called her son to tell him she was back and catch up on his news. He told her he was, "damned impressed with his old lady." Then she propped three pillows behind her and crawled into her bed. She sighed. Nothing feels as good as your own bed, she thought. She opened her tablet and began to read the newest James Hankins novel, ***A Blood Thing.***

Alphonso drove the Mean Machine into Marge's apartment and, as had become their custom, he handed her a bottle of wine as he drove through the door. She took it, bent and kissed the bald spot on top of his head. Marge's children, FBI and Chicago Police, said they weren't surprised. They assumed she had done most of the driving. They wouldn't trust anyone else but their mother behind the wheel of a Hummer pulling a trailer. When she told them about Betsy's trial they laughed and said again, they weren't surprised. After all, Betsy's cousin was their 'Ma'.

Robbie, without children to call, put on her summer robe, rubbed beautifully smelling cream on her legs and arms, also propped up three pillows and crawled into bed with her little bear and phone. Her call was answered on the first ring. "Hey, Raven," she said with a smile as she settled into the softness of the pillows.

Mary Rose's four daughters all fussed and said she shouldn't have gone and she didn't dare do anything stupid like that again. Mary Rose had the same reply to each one, "My dear, I'll do what I damn well please, and I came home with a beautiful Inukshuk." When they asked, always in angry voices, what an Inukshuk was, Mary Rose gently pushed the 'end' button on her smartphone and laughed a rather wicked laugh.

Wiley followed Mary Rose to her apartment after dinner. It was still light outside, and they stood together on Mary Rose's balcony. Birds were chirping good nights in the big pine and oak trees. Somewhere in the distance a night hawk called. There was a gentle, warm breeze and it was one of those perfect summer nights that promised warmth and rain.

They stood at the balcony railing, looking out onto the grounds and trees. A moon would soon be lighting the area and little bats would circle the lights and make flitting shadows on the walks below.

“It’s so good to be home,” Mary Rose said. “It was quite a trip.”

“It was,” Wiley said. He turned toward Mary Rose, took her face in his hands and gave her the world’s most tender kiss. Then he lowered one hand, reached into his pocket and pulled out a tiny box from Jade City.

“Mary Rose McGill,” he said quietly. “I love you. Will you marry me?”

Love When You're Old

From: *The BOOB Girls, The Musical: Mary Rose and Wiley's song.*

Love when we're old is just like years ago.
Exciting and warm, with a quiet, gentle glow.
Love never stops though time may quickly pass.
All I'm wanting is time - for love to last.

Just when I thought my gallivanting days
were through.
All that lay before me was a tired, setting sun.
I turned around and saw your face.
I had another wish.

I used to think times of tenderness
were past and gone.
Eternal like a night without a dawn.
You took my hand. The feeling was real.
Now I'm wishing for many long years with you.
Love when we're old is like years ago.
Soft and warm with a gentle, quiet glow.

A Note from Joy

When I finished reading the last page of this book, where Wiley proposes to Mary Rose, my helpmate and sweet husband, Ted, asked what I hope you asked as well: "Does she say,' yes?'" Frankly, I don't know yet, but I'm asking you now to help me decide for BOOB Girls XI. Does she say, "Yes"? I want you to join the girls and me at Table 12. They need to stay in Omaha for the next adventure. So here are the details:

Right now, the working title for the next book is:
The Gun Found at Marks

When Mark, of Marks Bistro - the girls' favorite restaurant- pulled up a crabapple tree to expand the patio, an old, galvanized bucket came up with the roots. The bucket was filled with cement. When the cement was broken open, there, lying on the ground, was an old gun.
How did the gun get there?
Was the gun used in a murder?
If so, who is the murder victim?
Who is the villain of your dreams?
How can the girls be taken back to 19th century Omaha to solve the mystery?
What excitement do you want to the girls to find?

And - will Mary Rose say, "Yes"?

Let me know your ideas with an email to Joy.Johnson@msn.com.

I'll be waiting to hear from you, and if you send me ideas, I'll send you a free book to say thank you.

And if you aren't getting the blog the girls write each month, email me and let me know and I'll get you on the list.

Ted and I really did drive the Alcan in our motorhome. He is 79 and I'm 80. For 11 months I'm older than he, so I say I'm his cougar and he's my arm candy, boy toy. It was a fabulous and tiring trip. We left in August and on October 1st we pulled into our winter home at Travis Air Force Base near San Francisco and the wine country. Ted writes a nice Christmas letter and when I read the last paragraph, I said, "This makes me tired!" We drove 12.000 miles in our motorhome, 5,000 miles more in our jeep, were in 20 major cities and 10 national parks and we visited 52 family members and friends in 2017. And yes, I brought home an Inukshuk and we gave Ulus as Christmas gifts.

This was the year of the horrendous California wildfires, and we were surrounded by the smoke from them. Planes from Travis left every day to turn into fire-fighting aircraft. There was so much destruction and sorrow. Just as the girls felt lucky after their trip, we feel lucky as well. And I am so grateful for YOU. Help me with ***BOOBs XI: THE GUN FOUND AT MARKS.*** The Burned Out Old Broads and I want your ideas.

Thank You!

An exotic Chicken Dinner in a romantic restaurant to my husband, Ted Brown. People are always asking him if he reads the books. With this one, he was an important part of the writing. I wrote every morning, then read what I wrote aloud to Ted. When I finished, and began the final tweaking, he sat beside me, read it over my shoulder and made really good changes. It was the kind of partnership every couple wants.

A tender slice of white meat to Janet Roberts, my genius daughter who has formatted all the books, designed the covers, hosted the launch parties and been a BIG part of the success of the series. She has taken over leadership of our non-profit bereavement center, Centering Corporation, and is doing a great job. As she used to say when she was a little girl, "I'm proud to you."

Let's make it a chicken-fried steak to Rev. Dr. James Campbell, my old friend and muse who told us the stories of the little town we turned into Gospel Bird, who lined us up with Mark Merrill, a true historian, and who is there when we need him, no matter what. We have what is true friendship and we are both lucky.

Hot Wings with just the right bite to Gloria Sorenson proofreader extraordinaire who has found something to change on every page. I swear that if I ever write a full page without Gloria's red pen marking it up, I will frame it and give it to her for Christmas. This is the proofreader you want - because of Gloria, I am free to just write. She takes care of the rest.

A giant drumstick to Ken (Kenny) Cusino who inspired Ken David David and, just as he moved everything from Hadley's old computer to her new one, Ken is my techie and my web master. Go to www.theboobgirls and enjoy his magic. He and his wife Denise are Ted's and my surrogate children, and we get together from 60 miles away, at least once a month and all four of us look forward to it for 30 days every time.

Best hamburger in the world to The Huns Den in Babb, just outside of Glacier National Park. There really is a sweet little boy who welcomed us, did arm wrestling with my husband, Ted, and won hands down. When I tried to call to tell them I wanted to put them in this book, the phone had been disconnected. I hope it's because the season is over, not that they've closed up shop. They really did advertise, and they really did have - the best hamburgers in the world.

An entire Gospel Bird to be shared by Rev. Dr. James Campbell and Rev. Dr. Harold Ivan Smith, the two wayward clergy who thought of the Fundamental Pentecostal Holiness Church of the True Baptism and the sermon written by Dr. Campbell. We church folk need to laugh at ourselves more, and if you think this is too sacrilegious, blame those two, who are good writers in their own right. The three of us all wrote grief books and Harold Ivan's book, Eleanor - about Eleanor Roosevelt, is headed for becoming a classic, and all of Jim's books are good reads.

Enough Gospel Bird bones to make a rich soup stock to Mark Merrill, who hosted Ted and me when we wanted a history of the Romanov's and to see the mines around what would become the village of Gospel Bird. Mark has wonderful stories of the Iditarod and area history and he became one of the highlights of our Alaskan adventure. Thanks, Mark!

A Poodle Puppy to John Suter, Poodle Man of the Iditarod. Go to YouTube and search for either John Suter or Poodle Man of the Iditarod and you'll see a delightful interview with John and Johnny Carson. Other great sites to search for are Inuksuks and the Signpost Forest.

A Big Bucket of Gospel Bird and two bottles of good wine to these BOOB Girls who shared ideas for the plot. As far as I know, it's the only series where the readers have an important part of the writing and you all deserve a standing ovation. Rebecca Villeneuve, Linda (Nancy Drew) Adams, Lin Braddy, Linda Alford, Cathy Nichols, Jane Dugan, Maureen O'Donnell, VIcky Dovenspike, Pat Callone, Kathleen Braza, Shirley Ring, Pat Wagner and her son, Steve.

The BOOB Girls Tour –
where they've been in all the books

Wolf Brothers Western Store, where Wiley went to buy a new western sport coat, was one of my late husband Marv's favorite places to shop. Located at 70th and Dodge, it's an old Omaha landmark with great stuff.

Metropolitan Community College (Metro) where Ken David David is going and where he met Denise has several campuses, but the most beautiful is at 5300 North 30th Street and was actually the old Fort Omaha, built in 1868. The Holland Center, where the gang went to hear the Omaha Symphony Pops concert, is at 13th and Douglas, an easy walk from the heart of the Old Market. The Holland is beautiful and has perfect acoustics. Two of my grandchildren have played there with the Omaha Area Youth Orchestra.

Prospect Hill Cemetery, where Anna Wilson and Dan Allen are buried is one of those best-kept secrets. Between 31st and 33rd Streets, bordered by Parker and Grant Streets, the cemetery hosts a reenactment each Memorial Day. It's a delight and the location is historic and beautiful. Residents of early Omaha used to picnic there on Sundays. It's worth a visit.

Nope, I'm sorry; there isn't a Salem's Crossing, Nebraska. Ben Schroeder, another surrogate grandson, loves Highway 30 so I let him set its location. He located it just North of Wood River which is two and a half hours west of Omaha just off I-80. Head there and you can see everything the girls saw and if you drive far enough, there's the Great Platte River Road Arch, Sandhill Cranes, Grand Island and America the Beautiful with amber waves of grain.

The Arboretum on Farnam Drive at 8141 Farnam, where I lived for three years, is just east of Methodist Hospital and, if you feel ambitious, you can park somewhere nearby and walk south on 84th Street to Pacific, turn right on Pacific and, in a short while, have coffee at **The Village Grinder.**

The Bookworm, where the girls browsed after coffee at The Grinder has moved. Get back on 84th, drive south to Center Street, turn right to 90th, then right again and you're at the new location. Go in and check to see how their supply of BOOB Girls books is holding up. The Bookworm is one of the finest independent bookstores you'll ever enjoy.

There really is a **Finicky Frank's** restaurant in Omaha and it's excellent. It's just off of I-680 at the 30th Street exit. Go north a very short way, turn left into a short road leading to the gas station and Finicky's. My favorite thing there is the breaded pork loin.

If you are coming from West Omaha, go to 105th and Pacific, then turn south until you find the beautiful **Happy Hollow Country Club** where Hadley has taken the group in nearly every book. Unless it's lunch or dinner time, you can probably find Kelly or Jim to show you the library, the girls' favorite room. Dorothy, who had worked at "Happy" for many years, died a few years ago. The place will never be the same. Drive on east to 72nd Street and turn left.

Now you're at the area where Morgan Graves furnished La Viva Crypt from the Lazy Leopard Lounge auction.

Keep driving north to 72nd and Maple. Turn left and you'll be at **Centering Corporation** at 73rd Street. This is the grief resource center Joy and Dr. Marvin Johnson founded in 1977. Drive into the parking lot, come in and say hello. Inside is Caring Cups Coffee Stop. We're waiting for you. After a cup of good Joe, visit Benson Plant Rescue next door and wander through our memory garden where you will be shaded by one of the grandest and oldest cottonwoods in Nebraska.

You'll leave Centering, turn right, then make a U-turn to head east again on Maple. Drive by or stop in Jane's Health Market and **Leo's Diner** in the village of Benson.

Continue on to 49th Street and turn right. At the corner of 49th and Happy Hollow, the house on your right - a lovely little English Tudor - belonged to Joy and Marv for more than 30 years. Keep driving and you'll be at the **Homy Inn** where the girls went for champagne on tap. As you drive across Happy Hollow, look to your right. At the end of the block, by what is lovingly called the traffic peanut, is Dan Simpson's Auto Shop. Danny found the hidden tracker in the Hummer in BOOB Girls V.

If it's near lunch time, turn right (South) at the Homy and go to the top of the hill to 51st Street. Turn left into the village of Dundee. Park where you can and walk to **Marks Bistro,** the girls' favorite restaurant at 51st and Underwood. If the weather is nice, have lunch on the most beautiful patio in Omaha. May I suggest Mark's famous Mac and Cheese, and ask for Mark. He'll be happy to say hello, show you Joy and Marv's booth - which is also Marge and her husband's - and the table where Warren Buffett met with Hillary Clinton.

After Marks, head south on 50th Street until you come to West Center Street. Turn left on Center and drive by **Kubat Pharmacy**, one of the few remaining family-owned pharmacies and where the girls bought the bedpan for Mary Rose's bedpan hat in BOOB Girls II.

Continue east on Center Street and you'll come to the Old Market. Now you're on your own. Visit **Wheatfield's, The Jackson Street Tavern, M's** and of course, **Ted and Wally's Ice Cream.** Stand beside the new Hyatt Place Hotel and look up at the third floor of the Mayfair Building across 12th Street. The apartment near the back by the fire escape was Joy and Marv's and Robbie's.

You'll be standing where Esmeralda sang her sad song to Robbie, then patted the beautiful horse in BOOB Girls III. Go into the Passageway where Wes and Hadley had dinner and go smell the leather at **Overland Sheepskin** where Wes bought a jacket. Keep walking east and you'll come to the former **ConAgra** campus and lake. If it's a nice day and you want to walk even more, the Bob Kerrey pedestrian bridge across the wide Missouri is just a little way north.

Now drive back on Center Street to 84th Street. Turn left on 84th and go to **Mangelsen's**, where you can find just about everything you need, including help making a bedpan hat.

Go south to Interstate 80 by Mangelsen's and head west. Drive to the Springfield exit and head south to Louisville. There you'll visit Coop de Ville on Main Street, the neatest little gift shop ever. Walk around the corner to the big white house and explore Feathers, the other gift shop decorated by Dr. Liz and her ladies. Have one of Dr. Liz's Scotcheroos and, like Robbie - buy a purse. It's sayings from the Coop bathroom that start the fifth book when Mary Rose looks in the mirror. "I do declare, I love my hair." That bathroom is worth a trip to Louisville anytime.

Get back on the highway by Louisville and drive a short distance to the sign reading South Bend. It's on Highway 66. If it's close to dinner time, head for **Round the Bend Steakhouse**, home of the Testicle Festival. Careful. Don't miss it, it's on your left and high on a hill.

After too much food at the Bend, go north until you get to I-80 again. Head west to exit 420. There is **Pine Grove RV Resort**, former home of Marv and Joy and where the girls went on their Staycation. Come in! Have a cup of coffee. Be sure to register at the office.

Go on to **Baker's Candies** in Greenwood and shop, shop, shop at the factory store. The gift shop is chocolate heaven.

You can dedicate an entire day to the **Henry Doorly Zoo**, where Marge and Alphonso had a date.

I'm sorry, but there is no **Meadow Lakes Retirement Community**. I picture it as being between Creighton University at 25th and California and the Old Market. There's no **Peyton's Hair Salon**, either. I picture it in one of the big apartment buildings near the river in the Old Market.

Ted and I are full time RVers at this time. We have a 34 foot motor home with three slide outs. One is a sunroom with four huge windows across the back, two on each side and four more in the ceiling. We call Omaha our home and, during the summer, we're at a place in Bellevue, Nebraska, called Base Lake, a very nice RV park that is part of Offutt Air Force Base. Ted was 25 years in the Air Force and one of my sweet possessions is a big red travel mug that reads, Air Force Wife. Base Lake is hard to find, but if you do, coffee is on us.

I also imagine I've left out some places. But if you want to follow the girls to Gospel Bird, Alaska, I'll be happy to direct you there.

Enjoy! And thank you for being part of Table 12.

Beginning of Joy and Ted's great adventure.

The Signpost Forest, Watson Lake, B.C.

Inukshuk:
The rock design created by
Artic Eskimos.

Ulu:
The ancient and completely modern knife
created by Eskimos.

Mary Rose's Inukshuk

Where the girls had the best hamburger!!

About the Author

Joy Johnson (Brown) is 80 years old now! With her late husband, Dr. Marvin Johnson, she founded Centering Corporation (www.centering.org), North America's oldest and largest bereavement Resource Center, and Grief's Journey, a Center for Grieving Children in Omaha, Nebraska. She has written or edited over 100 books on grief, many for children. After she retired from Centering Corporation in 2009, she began writing The ***BOOB Girls: The Burned Out Old Broads at Table 12.*** There are now ten books in the series.

Joy has three children and six grandchildren. Her marriage to Ted brought another son, daughter-in-law and granddaughter into her family. While she and Ted are still full-time RVers, their home base is Omaha, where most of the children live. She does at least thirty BOOB Girls talks each year.

If you enjoy this book, you'll love and laugh with:

The Boob Girls: The Burned Out Broads at Table 12

The Boob Girls II: Lies, Spies and Cinnamon Roles

The Boob Girls III: Sandhills and Shadows

The Boob Girls IV: Murder at Meadow Lakes

The Boob Girls V: The Secret of the Red Cane

The Boob Girls VI: From the Eye of the Moose

The Boob Girls VII: Ten Little Puritans

The Boob Girls VIII: Learning to Love Willie

The Boob Girls IX: The Boob Girls in Training Bras

The Boob Girls X: Gospel Bird

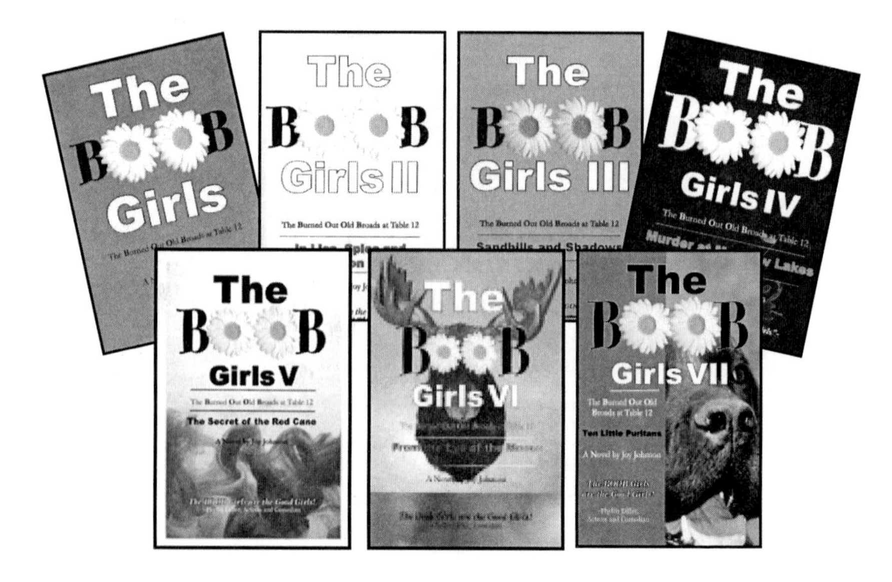

Now **YOUR** Community Playhouse Can Host *The BOOB Girls: The Burned Out Old Broads* **The Musical**

Now there is a new way to experience the delightful characters and offbeat adventures of "The Boob Girls." Adapted by innovative director and playwright Fran Sillau and award-winning composer Mark Kurtz, this musical comedy brings to the stage all the antics as well as tender moments from the book, along with exciting new songs, dances, and humorous entanglements. Your audiences will laugh till tears run down their legs.

The Tunes:

The BOOB Girl Theme
For the Rest of My Life, I'm Not Your Wife
None of that Kinky Stuff (Naked man in the Laundry Room Song)
It's Gonna Be Good: The Shopping Song
Just Look at Us and Beautiful
No Forwarding Address
Extortion is Sweet
Freedon!
The Family You Found
The Tattoo Song
I'm in Love with J Frederick Sapp
Argument
Polly's Song
The Adult Emporium Song
Wes and Hadley's Song
All Heart – the Hospital Song
We'll Remember
The BOOB Girl Song

For information about how your theater can produce this crowd-pleasing musical, please contact fran@fransillau.com.

Visit the girls and Joy Johnson at:

www.theboobgirls.com

www.welcometothe boobgirls.blogspot.com

Bring Some Joy to Your Group

Joy Johnson Brown speaks to over fifty groups each year with a humorous presentation on The Making of A BOOB Girl. Contact her for your state, national or local conference or meeting at joy.johnson@msn.com or through her website at www.theboobgirls.com.

To speak to her by phone, contact Centering Corporation at 866-218-101.